Middle Name M

Middle Name Misery

By Silius Creed

-Sigh-lee-us-

First Edition: November 2025
Published in the United Kingdom

Cover design by OpenAI's ChatGPT with creative direction by the author.

ISBN: 978-1-9192832-3-4
Author website: [SiliasCreed.co.uk]

Printed by Creed Noir Press
For more information, visit *Silias Creed* on Facebook.

Music Disclaimer

Filed under 'Emotional Evidence' in the Silias Creed Archive. Playback at your own risk.

Dedication

For Michele—
who leaves me to my own devices when I'm writing.
Does she know how my mind works?
Probably more than I do.
But she always knows
when Silias is in my head.

Acknowledgements

Writing is never a solitary act, no matter how many nights you spend talking to ghosts.

To Michele—your quiet patience and loud support are stitched into every fold of this book.

To my family, especially the ones who never roll their eyes (too much) when I vanish into noir fog or start muttering about glyphs and receipts over dinner.

To the readers who followed *She Walked In Like a Line of the Song* and came back for more—this is for you. You saw the signs. You trusted the silences. You let the train whistle.

To my late sister, Chris—your voice still echoes through these pages: in the laughs, the countdowns, and the childhood bogeymen.

And finally, to the ghosts in the Half Pint, and the ones watching from the riverbank: thanks for not leaving when the lights came on.

A Personal Note from Silias Creed

Some stories don't ask permission. They tap on the glass when you're half asleep, when your tea's gone cold, when the bins still haven't gone out and the cat's knocked something over for the third time. This one didn't knock. It slipped through the letterbox in a folded note and waited.

Middle Name Misery wasn't supposed to happen this soon. I'd planned a break—a breather. But Trixie, Goldie, Lola… they had other ideas. And Calder? Well. Some shadows just won't stay folded.

This book was written in stolen hours, in between the real world and the one that won't shut up. It's part love letter, part ledger. It hums with receipts, glances, half-spoken truths. I wrote it with a biro, metaphorically speaking, and there's probably still a fingerprint on every page.

If you've read this far—thank you. You didn't just read a story. You stepped into the bar. You watched the river. You folded the note and let it wait.

We're not done. Not by a long shot. But for now, let's sit with this one a while longer. Just until the train passes.

—Silias

Also by Silias Creed

She Walked In Like a Line of the Song
A noir novella about broken promises, louder jukeboxes, and the things left unsaid. Featuring Trixie Vane, Goldie Johnson, and enough smoke to fog a memory.

Knife Behind the Mirror
What you see isn't always what you get. The companion book that cuts deeper, stares longer, and folds sharper. Enter at your own risk.

The Creed Noir Companion: Vol. I (forthcoming)
Case notes, glyphs, receipts, and red herrings. The archive opens soon.

Foreword *(new direction)*

Some stories start with a bang.
This one starts with a receipt. Folded. Unopened. And passed from hand to hand like a secret no one wants to own.

Middle Name Misery is a tale written between silences. A noir of notes, debts, and the kind of women who don't flinch when the room gets quiet. If you've read *She Walked In Like a Line of the Song*, you'll already know the Half Pint. You'll know the girls. You'll know there are no heroes here—just timing, tension, and tea that never goes cold.

What you're about to read isn't just a sequel. It's a reckoning.
Not with violence. With silence.

Make yourself at home. But don't unpack.
This town doesn't keep guests long.

— Silias Creed

A Note on Elvis, and the Music That Built This

Before the ink. Before the names. There was *Fever.*

Elvis Presley's voice curled through a speaker one evening and lit a fuse I didn't know was waiting. The song wasn't loud—it didn't need to be. It just *knew*. And from that hush, came a world.

Middle Name Misery takes its title from *Trouble*. But the echoes run deeper—names like Goldie, Peggy, and Susan are lifted from lyrics (*Susan When She Tried*) and given new skin, new secrets. Every chapter hums with the rhythm of Presley's catalogue. Not always obvious. But always there.

This isn't an Elvis book. But it wouldn't breathe without him.

So, here's to the King.
For the spark. The soundtrack.
And the silence between the notes.

Author's Note

This one was slower to surface. Not because the story wasn't there—it always was—but because some folds don't open cleanly. *Middle Name Misery* isn't about action. It's about the echo after. The debt that doesn't get paid. The names that don't get written until they burn through the page.

Trixie, Goldie, Lola—they're louder now. Sharper. I knew from the start this was their book, not mine. I was just the one scribbling margins and folding receipts. If *She Walked In Like a Line of the Song* was a dance at closing time, then this is what happens after the jukebox cuts out and the room stops pretending it's fine.

Every chapter was written with a glass nearby—sometimes scotch, sometimes silence. Sometimes both. And if there's grit in the glamour, that's because I've learned the shine never lasts without it.

To the reader: thanks for walking these wet streets with us.
To the ghosts: I see you. Still.

— **Silias Creed**

PS There's a playlist tucked at the back. It doesn't explain the story, but it knows where the bodies are buried. Play it while you read—just keep the volume low. Silence still owes us something.

Chapter 1 — Fever

The bar is holding its breath again. It does that when it remembers who owns it. Not the landlord, not the breweries, not the men with full wallets and empty rings—no. The room belongs to whoever can make silence feel expensive.

Tonight, that's Trixie.

She doesn't walk to the mic so much as stand where the light decides to find her. A slim slice across her cheekbone, the kind of cut a streetlamp would make if it learned restraint. The air has thickened since the first set—smoke looping its lazy eights, a murmur like coins in a pocket. Then nothing. The hush comes down like a theatre curtain, and you can hear the barman wipe a glass in the wrong direction.

The bass starts. Two notes to say we're awake, a third to decide who we are tonight. It's that old heartbeat we stole from a record and taught to misbehave—found in a rehearsal when the electrics blew and all we had was a drum case and nerve. Walk, don't run, it tells the room. Confess, don't preach.

Across the floor, Goldie sits at the bar, profile like a postcard of trouble you send to yourself. She's not smiling, not exactly—just that half curve that says she knows the ending and she's letting you catch up. The barman lights a cigarette he's not supposed to sell any more. At the back, a woman watches the way people do when they're counting what a voice can take from a room. She doesn't move. She doesn't clap first. She lets silence do the measuring. She watches like people do when they're deciding if they've met you before—in a dream, in a lie, or at a crossroads you both took different ways from. I can't tell yet what she sees in Trixie: a warning, a rival, or a version of herself with the safety off.

Trixie raises her hand to shoulder height and snaps once. It's a small sound, but the bar rearranges itself around it. Another snap, a fraction to the right, and the room learns it has two ears. If you've got headphones on, the drums are already behind you, walking left to right like a ghost that likes to pace. She leans into the mic. Doesn't touch it. The trick is to make the mic come to you; she treats sound the way she treats men—tame it, seduce it, threaten it, but never chase it. "Never knew how much I love you," she says, not sings, the love landing like a secret she regrets telling. "Never knew how much I care." There's movement near the doormen who thought they were only here for beer remembering they're made of other things.

By the time you give me fever finds its way out of her throat, the light has decided to be kind. The bass grows a spine. The drummer—if you can call a set of brushes a man—licks the snare like a match and we're in it: the hunt. The rhythm goes around the walls, testing hinges.

She doesn't rush the verses. She walks them like a mean dog past a butchers. The room follows two steps behind, pretending not to beg. Romeo and Juliet show up late and leave earlier than they should. Someone at a table near the back laughs the wrong laugh and loses the right to speak for the rest of the song.

At the bar, a lighter clicks. Trixie hears it. So does everyone who knows what a cue looks like. She lets the silence breathe for the length of a heartbeat she once owed somebody, then turns her head enough for the light to ride her jawline. "Thou givest fever when we kisseth," she says, and the smile that curls after kisseth commits more crimes than the courts could process in a week.

Goldie's fingers tap once on the stem of her glass: three quiet beats to say proud. The woman doesn't move and that's the point. The barman has stopped wiping a glass midway, holding it like a stunned witness. A man in a football top mouths Christ without sound, then stares at his hands like they've betrayed him.

The bridge isn't a bridge so much as a stairwell that doesn't bother with the top step. The drummer's ghost goes right to left this time. Two men at a corner table shift in synchrony and think no one sees them. Everyone does. The barman's towel stops, mid wipe, like it just remembered a name.

Trixie drops her voice on "Captain Smith and Pocahontas" until we're all leaning forward to hear whether history apologizes. It doesn't. She makes that sound like a kindness. Then she climbs—it's not high, but from here it looks like a cliff—and for a second you remember the first time you wanted someone to be bad for you and hoped they were good at it.

She doesn't milk the last chorus. She owns it. The snaps sharpen, the bass grows its second heartbeat, and the air goes sticky with a heat that isn't from the ducts. On the word burn she doesn't sing; she exhales. A candle in reverse. A promise that knows exactly how to keep itself.

The three endings:

- The first lands soft. "What a lovely way… to burn." A confession said as if she's checking the time—for the romantic and the forgiven.
- The second is for the ones who flinched. "What a lovely way…"—and she lets the lovely run its finger along the table's edge— "…to burn." For the guilty who needed it said twice.
- The third is the warning. No smile. Just the motor of the word turning over. "What a lovely way…"—you can hear a glass set down across the room and whoever set it down knows they set it down— "…to burn." For the ones who don't listen until the smoke gets in their lungs.

Silence. Real, good, paid for silence. The applause arrives late—proper applause always does, because it has to beat a spell before it claps. Goldie breaks it first, like a door opened from the inside—sharp, unhurried. The woman at the back follows a heartbeat later, palms together in a rhythm that says she's thinking about hands, and what they're for.

Men who came to shout at football screens clap because they've remembered they have hands and want forgiveness.

The barman smiles the smile people wear when they've seen better nights and just got given one.

Trixie doesn't bow. She doesn't do bows. She steps back from the mic the way you step back from a lit stove you intend to use again in five minutes. Someone whistles. It isn't her. She looks in that direction until it stops.

I don't clap. I don't anymore. There are moments you applaud and moments you keep—the good ones are both and neither. I watch the smoke pattern what she just did to us and think about all the names for heat: fever, hunger, mercy, ruin. Some of them rhyme and some of them don't. None of them apologize.

She turns her face fractionally toward me and I can read the question there the way some men read racing sheets. Are we clear? Not about the song. About the room. About the promise it just made to her but hasn't written down yet. Someone will try to cash it. Someone will try to break it.

"We're clear," I say, to nobody. The bass player nods like we shook hands in a dream. The brushes rest.

At the far end of the counter, a lone man fails at lighting a cigarette with dignity. Goldie lays a coin on the bar and taps it twice—I'll handle him. The womans shadow slips off the wall like it's learned to walk. The room holds its breath one last time, then finally lets it out—not just lungs, but shoulders, secrets, the little lies people tell themselves about why they came. The bar exhales and remembers its own size.

On her way past, Trixie taps the microphone with the back of a finger. The small thump goes out into the speakers and comes back as a doctrine: the soft things are the ones that carry.

"You don't just sing the fever," I say, once I'm sure nobody is listening. "You are the fever."

The room nods without meaning to. Then somebody laughs and the spell becomes a story people will lie about being present for. The night moves on, as if it hadn't already been marked.

Chapter 2 — Trouble

The room's half a fight already—glasses too full, men too loud, that sweet edge where laughter wants to turn into something it can't apologise for later.

Trixie steps up like she's collecting a debt. Boots planted. Mic low. No patter. The bass gives a curt one-two; the drummer answers with brushes that sound like a fuse being considered.

"If you're looking for trouble—" she says it like a favour she doesn't owe. The smile has teeth. The room tilts toward her the way rooms do when they decide who they belong to.

Goldie holds the bar like a line in the sand. At the back, the problem pretends to be a table.

Trixie doesn't go loud; she goes close. Guitar on a leash—Tele bite tucked behind her shoulder, all attack, no bark. The tempo leans forward without rushing. You can feel the song reconsider the room, then pick up its feet anyway.

Second verse, she steps left and the lights come with her like trained animals. She doesn't look at the back yet. She looks at the women—two by the door, one by the jukebox—and lets them have the warning before the men do. That's manners.

Middle eight—she raises two fingers and snaps once. The band drops to breath only. You could count the coins in the till. Someone does. The problem laughs once, wrong note, then remembers his drink.

She turns just enough for the back to borrow her eyes for a second. Not a threat. A calendar reminder.

"If you're looking for trouble—" softer now, heavier anyway.

The words arrive under the ribcage where names live.

I watch the room do arithmetic: laughter minus distance; distance minus nerve; nerve minus witness.

She rides the last chorus like a slow wave, then snaps again—a ghost of sound—and lets the final line fall off the mic, unamplified, bar-quiet. It carries farther than it has any right to. A glass decides to stop being vertical. Nobody claps until it lands.

Silence. Real, good, paid-for silence. Then applause comes in clean, like a decision.

She doesn't bow. Doesn't wait. She leaves the mic where it is and walks past the back table so close the problem has to choose between breathing in and learning something.

Goldie taps the bar twice as she goes by—metronome, message. The band looks like it just got away with something.

We don't stay for an encore. Watch. Listen. Leave.

Chapter 3 — The Whistle Scene

The rain had the decency to stop five minutes after it mattered. The alley behind the Half Pint steamed like a kettle, brickwork sweating under the streetlamp's tired flicker. Neon coughed, undecided.

He waits where cowards do—half in shadow, half in someone else's mistake. Cheap aftershave. Cheaper nerves.

Trixie doesn't rush. The door sighs shut behind her. A match rasps; flame kisses her knuckle, then the cigarette. She studies the smoke like it's the weather report. The lamp tries to steady when she speaks; it does.

"You're late," he says, aiming for hard and landing on hollow.

"I'm right on time," she says. "You're just new to clocks."

He tries a laugh. It dies between his shoes.

"Whatever you think you heard in there," he says, "you heard wrong."

"That so?" She finds the only dry patch with her heel. "I heard you say a name that isn't yours. And I heard a promise your pockets can't afford." Her eyes flick once past him, to the fire-stairs door and its peeling biscuit advert—the kind kitchens use when they keep their secrets in tins.

He takes a half-step. The lamp buzzes like a fly on a bruise.

Down the line, a train throws two notes and is gone; the alley keeps the echo.

"Don't," she says—quieter. Quieter pulls him in. "Here's what happens. You tell me who paid you to talk. You tell me where they keep the tape. And you tell me why I shouldn't walk back in, finish my drink, and let this town eat the rest of you."

He swallows. Loud. "You don't scare me."

"Good," she says. "Fear makes men noisy. I prefer quiet. Quiet's where I do my best work."

Silence finds them. A glass breaks somewhere inside; the bar pretends not to listen.

"You're not calling anyone?" he asks.

"No." She taps ash into a puddle—small fireworks. "In an hour—set a clock, teach yourself the trick—you're going to call yourself and say you did the right thing. For once, it'll be true."

He squares up, last scrap of bravado. "You can't make me—"

Trixie steps just close enough to count his heartbeat. Lowers her voice half an inch. "You know how to get someone to listen, sugar? You don't raise your voice. You lower it. Make 'em lean in."

He leans. He can't help it.

"And when they lean in," she says, the cigarette's cherry a small red moon, "that's when you cut them off at the knees."

He breaks first. They always do. "Door under the fire stairs. Second lock's busted. Tape's in a biscuit tin behind the till."

"Good lad." Two fingers tap his chest—no bruise, enough mark. "Forget my name until you've earned it."

"You think you're some kind of warning?"

She drops the butt, grinds it slow. "Darlin'," she says, turning for the door, "I am the whistle."

The lamp holds steady long enough to watch her leave, then thinks better of it and falters.

Chapter 4 — Old Leigh Cockles

Old Leigh has the kind of honesty I respect: it smells like what it is. Brine, diesel, vinegar, a hint of rot that doesn't apologize. Nets drip. Boots thud. A length of rope slaps a post in tired applause; the bait fridge hums a square breath of cold air that smells like last week. The gulls work their shifts, screaming union rules into the grey. The tide thinks about coming back and decides to sulk a little longer.

Trixie takes the paper tray from the hatch like a queen accepting tribute. Steam lifts off the cockles and makes a soft halo she refuses to notice. She doesn't look up at me—I'm background today, a shadow with pockets—but I catch the flick of her eyes towards the sheds. Goldie leans on a post near the waterline, arms folded, pretending to mind the estuary. She's watching everything.

Our contact is late enough to be rude and early enough to be nervous. Widow's jacket, fisherman's cap, hands like old rope. She calls herself Mags. Old Leigh knows her as Maggie Dot—white-dot headscarf, quick with vinegar, quicker with memory.

"Vinegar?" the girl in the hatch asks.

"Drown 'em," Trixie says, without taking her eyes off Mags.

The girl obliges. It's a murder the vinegar is proud of.

"Walk with me," Mags says. It isn't a question. Trixie lifts the tray, gives me a glance that means *stay wide*, then drifts along

the row of tarred timber, past the signs that used to mean something to men who are almost all dead now.
I let a couple with a pushchair and a dog cut me off, then take the outside. I want the van that will arrive before we're finished. There's always a van. Leigh runs on vans and gossip. I prefer to arrive first; if it looks at Trixie the wrong way, I prefer to be in the way.
Mags keeps her hands in her pockets. "You didn't come alone," she says.
"I never do," Trixie says. She spears a cockle with the little wooden fork and eats it like a secret. "Talk quiet. The gulls don't keep counsel."
"You were right about the name." Mags keeps her face forward. "It isn't on the paperwork, but it's on the tongues. Hartley. Sometimes Mr. Hart if someone wants to sound like they're not afraid."
Trixie nods like the tide did. She works in tides—wait, move, take. "Where?"
"Lock-ups by the bridge. The old units behind the chandlery. Number twelve—painted over twice, still peels."
"And the thing we asked you for?" Trixie says, like she's asking about weather.
Mags tips a river of vinegar onto the tray for show. Her other hand—a magician's hand, the honest kind—slides a folded, greasy napkin under the rim. Trixie doesn't look down. People who look down get seen.

"Two nights a week they move boxes after hours," Mags says. "Same van, same driver. No plates on the front, dent on the side." She checks the air like it owes her rent. "They're careful. Not careful enough."

"Who paid you to notice?" Trixie asks.

"No one," Mags says. "Who paid me to remember is your business."

We pass Goldie. She doesn't move, doesn't blink, but the corner of her mouth raises a fraction—the signal for *company incoming*. I hear it a second later: Transit engine, cough that never got serviced. The van noses onto the frontage like a stray dog that's learned to open bins. White paint, never washed. Right side panel puckered like it lost a fight with a bollard.

A man gets out wearing a borrowed smile that hangs a little crooked, like he stole it off someone braver. He throws it at Goldie first because men always throw the good china at the person who will break it. She gives him the look that ends most small lives.

"Name," Trixie says to Mags, not stopping. "First will do."

Mags swallows like the word is sharp. "Calhoun. Or Callan if he's pretending to be softer."

"Which is he today?"

"Depends who's watching."

"Everyone," Trixie says.

We hit the corner by the bait fridge. Trixie finally checks the napkin. Vinegar has smudged the pencil into a small storm: Unit 12, behind Belgrave Chandlery. Keysafe under guttering. Code: 1958. HARTLEY / CALHOUN. There's a sketch of a turn that only a person who's nearly been hit by a van would draw. It reads like a map and a warning—maybe a confession written to be eaten.

"Nice year," I say. She knows which song I mean.

"Later," she says. "Let the year wait."

Behind us, the van man tries a line on the girl in the hatch. She laughs like a good liar: convincing and kind. Goldie peels off from the post, slow as mercy, and ghosts along the curb to block his view of Trixie and Mags. It's a small move. It's enough.

"What do you want for this?" Trixie asks Mags, stopping in the wind shadow of a shed. Mags's cap looks older here. So does she.

"Nothing I'll get," Mags says. "But I'll take the thing I can. You don't bring this trouble back to Leigh."

Trixie holds her gaze. "We never bring it. We just follow it to where it sleeps."

Mags doesn't smile. "Then wake it somewhere else." She fades sideways into a knot of men smoking the slow tobacco you roll yourself; their smoke smells like work and weather. She leaves behind a different air—the quick, citrus perfume of girls photographing each other's cones on the quay. Boots in one direction, heels in the other. Old Leigh keeps both accounts. Goldie rejoins us with a question in her eyebrow. Trixie answers it by tucking the napkin into my pocket and tapping it once, like she's blessing a relic.

"Belgrave," I say. "Twelve."

"Tonight?" Goldie asks.

"No," Trixie says. "When the tide turns."

"Romantic," Goldie says, and looks out over the flats where the river pretends to be a sea. "You buying?"

"I already did," Trixie says, and steals the last cockle from the tray. She eats it without looking away from the van. The driver meets her eyes and looks down first. They always do.

We leave the sheds to their gulls and vinegar. Behind us, the van decides not to be brave. In front of us, the river shivers in its sleep. Somewhere between the two is a lock-up with a code that thinks 1958 was only about music. It wasn't. It was about debts, and doors, and the kind of names that stick to you in the dark.

Chapter 5 — Hadleigh Castle

The ruins sit on the ridge like a lesson nobody finished. Two broken towers, a spill of wall, the kind of grass that looks soft until it remembers rain. Down below, the estuary is a silver argument between river and sea. The pylons don't blink. Southend throws its lights down the coast like a dare—cheap promises of distant men. I file that; someone will make one before midnight.

We take the sheep-path, boots slick with the last shower. The wind needles at our ankles first, then climbs for the throat the higher we go, as if it wants a say in the conversation. Goldie goes first; hair pulled back in a knot that's more defiance than style. Trixie follows with her hands in her jacket pockets, the way you do when you don't trust the wind not to pick them.

"I thought it'd be bigger," Goldie says when we reach the top.

"It was," Trixie says. "Everything is, until somebody tests it."

There's shelter if you know where to stand—stone to your back, sky to your front, the ruined window making a picture frame out of the river. They take it without speaking. I hang to the side where the grass dips, not close enough to be company, not far enough to be missed if something goes wrong. Some nights you're the shadow that pays the bill.

For a while it's just the wind. It carries salt up the slope and dries nothing. A train threads the bottom of the hill and is gone again, leaving two notes that pretend to be a melody. The towers don't move. They've already moved as much as they're willing to.

Trixie lights a cigarette and doesn't smoke it. She holds it like a line she could cross. Goldie takes it off her and does the smoking for both of them. The ember ticks time on its own terms—burning without music.

"Remember when we used to come up here to nick kisses?" Goldie says, half-smile, eyes on the water.

"We used to come up here to not be seen," Trixie says. "Kisses were a by-product."

Goldie laughs once, the quiet kind. "You ever wish we'd left it there? Not been seen?"

Trixie's shoulders lift, then settle. "I'm no good at invisible."

"Liar," Goldie says, gentle. "You vanish when you want."

"Only when I need a witness," Trixie says.

They let that sit. A gull slides past at eye level like a sketch someone decided not to finish. The river has that late light on it that makes even mud look honest.

Goldie toes a piece of chalk from the soil and writes a small, crooked X on the stone by her hip. "Here," she says. "So, we know where we were when we stopped pretending."

Trixie looks at the mark. "We never pretended."

"We always pretended," Goldie says. "Just not about the same thing at the same time."

I've watched them pretend different things for years: that danger is a hobby, that loyalty is easy, that love behaves if you feed it on schedule. I know my role. I'm not the alibi. I'm the witness.

The cigarette burns itself clever. Trixie takes it back and kisses the filter like she's sealing a letter. "Say it plain," she says.

Goldie doesn't hurry. She breathes in, then out, and leaves a fog on the air that the wind tears to ribbons. "I hate that I love you more when you're on a stage," she says. "And I hate that you need the stage to love me back."

Trixie doesn't wince. Not outwardly. She leans on the window edge until the stone decides it knows her. "That's not fair."

"It's true," Goldie says.

"True isn't fair," Trixie says. "Fair is for games."

Down the ridge a dog barks at nothing that can be prosecuted. The towers keep their counsel. Somewhere behind us, a car door closes and reconsiders. We're alone again. The wind tries too hard for a moment—grabs hair, steals words—then, like it's embarrassed, drops back to a job it understands.

"You think this breaks us?" Goldie asks, voice steady. "The thing we're chasing. The man with too many names. The girls who swear they don't know him."

Trixie rolls her head side to side as if loosening a song. "Everything breaks us," she says. "That's why we carry spares."

Goldie lets the wind push hair loose from the knot. A strand sticks to her mouth; she doesn't move it. "So why here?" she says. "Why bring me up to the end of a wall to talk about us like we're just another ruin?"

Trixie's eyes go to the estuary, following the thin bright seam where the sun has the last word it never keeps. "Because this place remembers what it is after losing what it was," she says. "And because if I said this in the bar, you'd think it was part of the act."

She turns then, all the way, and the wind stops trying so hard. "I don't need a stage to love your back," Trixie says. "I need a witness. There's a difference."

Goldie looks at her, and there's a long road of history in the not-speaking. "Be careful," she says at last. "I'll hold you to that."

"Hold me to the end of it," Trixie says.

From where I stand, I can read the rest of the sentence she doesn't say. *If there is one.* The day is thin now. Canvey's lights come on like the cheap promises of distant men. The shriek of a train gives us a grace note. I keep the tune—openings, endings.

Goldie pockets the chalk. "What happens when we find him?" she asks. "Hartley. Hart. Calhoun. That lot."

"We stop him from borrowing our names," Trixie says. "We make sure the girls who swear they don't know him get to keep swearing."

"And then?"

Trixie exhales. The cigarette reaches its last inch, a small sun on parole. She pinches it out against the stone just as the vow begins—no band this time, just heat. "Then we go home," she says. "Or what passes for it."

Goldie steps closer until the wind doesn't fit between them. It isn't a kiss. It's the absence of one—and somehow louder. She rests her forehead against Trixie's for the length of a count-in.

"Swear it," Goldie says.

"I'll keep the shadows warm," Trixie says, soft enough to be a private oath. "Until you're back."

Warm how? I wonder. Shelter? Memory? Readiness? I don't ask. The wind already knows more than it tells.

Goldie closes her eyes. "And the question?"

"We leave it," Trixie says. "For now."

I can guess the shape of it: love, survival, the names we answer to when the lights go out. They don't need my answer.

They separate like professionals, not romantics: crisp, without apology, already looking at the path down. The X on the stone looks like a child's mark, which is maybe the point. The tide has turned somewhere we can't see yet. The wind finds its old job.

On the way back, Goldie threads her arm through Trixie's like the simplest things are the strongest ones. They don't look at me. They don't have to. Some nights, being trusted is the same as being invisible.

Below us, the river pretends to sleep. In the dark between the towers, a vow hangs in the air with enough weight to bruise, and enough mercy to keep walking.

Chapter 6 — Pie & Mash

Noon takes the edge off danger. Or pretends to. The pie & mash shop is all tile and ghosts of Mondays, parsley liquor fogging the window until the street forgets us—and what we owe it.

Trixie orders without looking at the board. "Double pie, mash split. Liquor heavy." Goldie says nothing, just taps the vinegar twice like she's setting a metronome.

We take a booth where the grout's gone grey—elbow-shined, truth-polished. Places like this collect confessions in the corners and stack them behind the salt.

Spoons clink. The queue breathes. A kid in a Hi-Viz drops two bottles of Dandelion & Burdock and blushes like he's broken a law.

Our contact slides in opposite—tabard, flour on the cuff, the faint warm smell of yeast and steam. He checks the door twice and rubs his wrist under the sleeve like he's unknotting a thought. Doesn't give a name.

A square of greaseproof peeks from under Trixie's plate like a tongue. It looks like the truth wants to speak but has been buttered quiet.

"Salt, pepper, truth," Trixie says, passing the shakers across.

He leaves them where they are and lifts the plate instead. The paper comes away with a soft kiss.

Written tight in pencil: "Belgrave: Tues/Thurs after close. Watch for anchor tattoo. Two knocks, one long. If it's Hartley, he won't look up."

Goldie tastes the liquor and decides it's honest—sharp-warm, parsley and tin, the flavour of a story that's been paid for.

I study the rhythm: two knocks, one long. Somewhere, someone decided that was the tune. Get it wrong and you get a lecture if you're lucky; a shut door if you're not.

Outside, the noon crowd swaps places with the afternoon. Inside, the steam hangs on a little longer, hiding edge as long as it can. We finish what's in front of us. Some days the work is meat and mash. Some days it's the word after watch.

Pie & Mash → Unit 12

By the time the parsley liquor stops steaming, noon has given back the edge it borrowed. We fold the greaseproof small—habit-size—and let the rhythm live in our fingers: two knocks, one long. Goldie reads the sky instead of a watch; she can tell when the light thins and the tide starts thinking about turning. Trixie doesn't look at clocks; she listens to rooms and waterlines. *When the tide turns*, she'd said at the sheds; she says it again now without words, just with the way her shoulders set to the street. I keep the year in my pocket—1958, cool and heavier than plastic has any right to be—and the train throws us two notes that ride the afternoon like a promise: warning or farewell, depends on the night.

Daylight had the decency to make us anonymous; night will take our side if we arrive first. Belgrave's back lot waits with corrugate ribs and numbers painted over until they forgot what they were. A sticker promises biscuits in a salt-air place—sweetness pretending. Rooms take sides. So do nights. When the river lets go of its breath, we move: Goldie to perimeter, me to keys, Trixie to the decision. Wait, move, take.

Chapter 7 — Unit 12 — Belgrave Chandlery

The tide turns like a held breath released. We take that as our cue; always did. The lock-ups behind Belgrave sit in a huddle, corrugate ribs, peeling numbers—12 has been painted over twice and lost both arguments. Sodium lights make the concrete colour of old teeth. Somewhere inland, a train throws two notes and leaves us the echo—warning or farewell or memory; depends on the night. Tonight, it sounds like Hartley's kind—brisk and borrowed—or something older that doesn't care about names.

Goldie walks the perimeter slowly, hands in pockets, counting cameras and sins. Trixie stands in the lee of a gutter, looking up like she's reading weather; her eyes find the keysafe tucked under the downpipe bracket. She doesn't smile. She doesn't need to.

"Year?" I say.

"1958," she says, polite to the box, like it's earned the attention. The buttons complain in plastic. The safe yields with a little indignation, the way cheap things do when asked to behave. She palms the key and drops the black shell back into its shadow.

Across the yard, a side door waits under a sheet of light. A sticker on it is half-peeled, selling biscuits nobody buys in shops like this; sweetness pretending in a salt-air place. Trixie notices. Of course she does. I try to remember if I still believe in sweetness; most days it pretends. Some nights it earns it.

"Two knocks, one long," Goldie says, barely a voice. "If we need it."

"We won't," Trixie says, and that's the kind of decision a tide makes.

Unit 12 opens on rope and oil. The air has a weight to it, like it's been asked to carry names. The torch stays cupped low in my hand, turning aisles of chandlery into a church that stocks anchors instead of hymns. Boxes stamped with places and numbers. A ledger on a nail by the office window; someone's tried to clean their fingerprints off it and only made them interesting.

Goldie slides behind the till like she was born there. She crouches, feels along the skirting, and pulls a floral biscuit tin that used to live in a grandmother's kitchen. The hinge squeaks a sentence. Inside: a cassette tape with no label, a USB stick that thinks it's modern, and a folded receipt with Hart written where Hartley didn't fit.

Footsteps. Not ours.

Trixie doesn't look up. She sets the tin back, empty, and tucks the goods under her jacket. In its place she leaves a twin tin we brought, filled with washers and nothing useful. Goldie ghosts away from the counter and is suddenly a shadow where a shadow should be.

The anchor tattoo arrives attached to a forearm and a man who breathes like a fridge. He pauses in the doorway as if his script got wet. He doesn't look up. Hartley's kind rarely do.

"Forgot my wallet," he says to the air, which is where men talk when they don't want to see answers.

Trixie steps into the spill of the side light like she belongs to it. Not near enough to be grabbed, near enough to be welcomed. "Happens," she says. "Some wallets don't like being kept."

He stops. The tattoo flexes once, the ship settling on its ink sea. "We're closed."

"Door was open," Trixie says, almost apologetic. "Two knocks, one long, wasn't it?" She raps the rhythm on the counter with a fingernail—two, one—like a woman reminding a song how it goes.

That buys us three seconds, maybe four. Enough for Goldie to drift past me, the cassette and the stick already where pockets make promises. I move to where I can be in the way if being in the way becomes required.

"You with the chandlery?" he says, trying to decide whether to use a name. He doesn't. Names are invoices.

"I'm with whoever keeps their tins tidy," Trixie says, and lets her eyes flick once to the floral on the shelf behind him. He crosses his arms to hide the tattoo. That tells me what he thinks is evidence.

Somewhere outside, a gust tries the door and fails. The wind's good at its job again. The train's echo fades to the sort of silence you can spend.

He shifts weight. "We're closed," he says again, like repetition is security.

"And yet," Trixie says, softer, "here we are."

The quiet thickens. He doesn't step forward. He doesn't look up. He does the thing men do when their script runs out: he reaches for the room to back him. The room doesn't. It's with us tonight. Rooms take sides; you learn to hear which way the walls are leaning.

“Tell Hartley,” Trixie says—gentle enough to pass for kind—“that a woman with a quiet voice asked him to stop borrowing names that aren’t his.”

His jaw ticks: his eyes flick once to the floral tin. He clocks the word borrow and chooses not to be offended. That tells me he knows the rate of interest.

We’re done. Trixie backs toward the door without turning, the way you leave a sleeping dog who might wake helpful. Goldie is already outside, flaming a lighter like she’s been there a year—a small signal, not a threat; a promise we’re finishing what we started. I lock up with the same courtesy I used to get in.

As we step into the yard, the sodium light decides to flicker, then remembers itself. The tide has finished turning. The air feels like a bill paid to the exact penny.

“Walk,” Trixie says, and we do. On the way out the order is different: watch, listen, leave. Past the peeling 12, past the gutter that tried to hide a key, past the sticker that wants you to believe in biscuits.

"Nice year," I say, because I can't help myself.

"Later," she says. "Let the year wait."

We take the long way out, through the shadow of a mast painted on corrugate. The train gives us two notes more, like a curtain call for people who don't bow. In my pocket, the cassette edges my knuckles—cool, heavier than plastic has any right to be. It feels like 1958 wasn't just about music. It was about the cost of getting heard.

Chapter 8 — Lola, Spelled Slow

She steps out of the quiet like it owed her money. Bruised-silver hair catching what little light the room kept for itself. No hurry. No apology.

The barman blinks like a man remembering a name too late.

She rests two fingers on the counter. "I'm looking for the woman who doesn't raise her voice," she says—not loud, not soft. "Tell her I'm not here to waste air."

Goldie tilts her head, smile with no decision in it yet. "And you are?"

The woman taps the wood once, checking it for secrets. "Lola," she says. Then she writes it in the air with the same mouth. "L. O. L. A." A beat. "Lola."

The room tries the name on. It fits.

Trixie doesn't turn straight away. She lets the syllables come to her like the mic does. When she looks, it's two mirrors finding each other in a narrow hall.

"Names are cheap," Trixie says. "Keeping them isn't."

The barman remembers how to breathe. Someone at the back forgets to finish their drink.

We learn the shape of the name and decide to keep it.

Chapter 9 — The Back Room Doesn't Blink

You can tell a place by its back room. Not the one they show you on a tour, the other one—the real room, where the kettle hisses like it knows too much and the chair limps when it thinks no one's looking.

We're in one of those. Not new, not safe, but ours for the hour. The tiles on the wall hold the heat like a memory they didn't ask for. The window's jammed half-open and smells of somebody else's decisions.

Goldie leans against the fridge like she invented casual. Her hair's up, but not tidy, like it got bored halfway through the plan.

Trixie sits cross-legged on the counter, boots still on, tapping a rhythm on the cupboard door like she's daring it to answer back.

"Still think we should've run the plates," Goldie says.

"No," Trixie replies, without looking. "Running plates means we're chasing. I don't chase."

"You don't run, full stop."

"I delegate the running."

The fridge hums like it's heard better jokes.

Goldie flicks the kettle switch off, then on again. It clicks like a threat. "If Calder shows early..."

"He won't," Trixie says. "He likes an entrance."

"He'll get a receipt."

"He'll get a reckoning."

The kettle doesn't boil. It sulks instead.

Goldie moves to the window, shifts the frame with a practiced hand. "We've done back rooms before," she says. "This one's quieter."

Trixie slides off the counter and crosses the room. Not quick. Not slow. The space just rearranges to let her through.

They meet in the middle, where the linoleum floor has given up pretending to be anything but tired. No soundtrack. No need.

Goldie touches Trixie's shirt, smooths a wrinkle that isn't really there. "You put this on inside out."

"I know."

"Statement or accident?"

"Both."

Goldie smirks, but it's soft. "You always did like a contradiction."

"And you always noticed."

There's a pause that isn't awkward—just full. Trixie leans in, and their foreheads touch before anything else. It's not a kiss, not quite. It's the moment before one. A breath they borrow together.

Outside, a car door slams. The fridge stops humming. The kettle finally clicks.

They pull apart like professionals. No guilt, no rush. Just the job walking back into the room.

Trixie checks her watch. “Time?”

“Borrowed,” Goldie says.

Trixie nods, ties her hair up with a band she finds in her pocket. “Then let’s spend it like it cost something.”

They don’t speak again until the door opens, and the light from the corridor decides who it’s here for.

Chapter 10 — Playback

We take the upper deck because rooms take sides and the sky hasn't picked one yet. The heater breathes like an old dog under the dash. I fish the tape player out of the glovebox—a charity-shop survivor with a temper—and feed it the cassette that's been heavy in my pocket since Belgrave. The plastic clicks. The heads clear their throat. Hiss taxes the words before we've even earned them.

Goldie wipes a porthole in the condensation with her sleeve. Trixie sits still enough to make the wind do the moving for her.

"Ready?" I ask.

"Play it," she says, voice half a key lower than usual. Performance is over; work's on.

Leader tape, then a scrape like a chair leg on concrete. Forklift beep somewhere far. Two men. One calls the other Hart but never looks up. The other says Callan, then Calhoun when he thinks no one caught it. Borrowed names trying on each other's coats.

"Tuesday, Thursday after close," a voice says, bored enough to be dangerous. "Same load. Unit twelve. Code stays. Same van. No plates front." A knuckle on metal—must be the till. Someone laughs without teeth. I picture what it carries: truth, bodies, borrowed names—whatever travels light.

A gust shoves the car and eats a sentence we'll want later. Rooms take sides; tonight, the wind votes against us. Goldie tightens her jaw like she can bully air.

I tap pause, rewind with a pencil, let the wobble settle. The tape wants to be heard; it just wants paying first. I'm responsible for the carrying, not the content—get it out clean, get it home.

Different slice. New air. You can hear outside this time—gulls and a low engine. "Wall past the sea road, last lay-by, Wednesdays," the bored voice says to someone we don't hear. "Same van. No plates front. Don't look up." The last line lands like a habit, not a rule.

Trixie tips her head a degree. "He drills them on not looking up," she says. "Teaches men to be furniture."

"Easier to move," Goldie says.

There's a woman in the background now. Doesn't speak. You only know because a lighter clicks and someone breathes more carefully. I wonder if she knows the shape of the thing she's standing inside, or if she's just learned to breathe carefully whenever men start naming each other. A door opens. The forklift beep gets closer and the steel-on-steel rings like a bell in a church that owes tax.

The player coughs. The tape chews a little and thinks better of it. I ease the spool with a thumbnail, and we get one more run.

"—Hale," someone says too fast, like they tripped on a name and pretended it was a step. "Mr Hart said—" The rest drowns under a compressor kicking in. Rooms turn on you. They do it without shame. They don't mind who pays.

"That enough?" I say.

"It will be," Trixie says. "Wall past the sea road. Last lay-by. Wednesday." She doesn't write it down. People who write it down get seen.

Goldie leans back, eyes on the sodium orange bouncing off the windscreen. "Hale, Hart, Callan, Calhoun," she says. "Pick a card." She doesn't look like she wants to pick; she looks tired of the deck.

"They're all the same card," I say. "Just different corners bent."

We sit with it a while. The heater ticks itself into a better mood. It doesn't warm us; it just reminds us we're cold. Out beyond the car park edge, a train throws two notes into the dark and keeps the third for itself. Tonight, they sound like older business—the kind that doesn't care what men call themselves as long as they arrive on time.

"Watch," Trixie says, like she's tuning the air. "Listen. Leave."

We do.

Chapter 11 — Sea Wall Layby

The last lay-by past the sea road looks like a place the map forgot to spell properly. A low concrete lip, a blue bin that's seen more wind than rubbish, and a view of water pretending to be brave. Sodium lights do their old-tooth glow. Out on the flats a train throws two notes and keeps the third like a private joke—two for us, the third kept back, like the train knows a punchline we don't—promise or warning; tonight, it sounds older than Hartley's lot.

We're early. We are always early. The heater stays off so the windows don't breathe for us. Trixie kills the interior light with a thumbnail; Goldie cracks her window a fraction and tests the wind like a sommelier. Salt, diesel, a memory of fried food from the caravan that isn't here at night.

"Watch, listen, leave," Trixie says, a count-in instead of a speech.

Goldie taps the thermos lid twice and passes it forward. Coffee would be a lie; what's inside is hotter and less honest. I let the cup fog the glass in a small circle and wipe it with my sleeve until the world returns in sodium and grey.

The road gives us a handful of cars that mind their own evenings. Then the van comes, shouldering the wind like it believes in itself. No front plates. Right-side dent, puckered like a bad memory. It rolls past, brakes without the courtesy of lights, and reverses into the lay-by until its doors become the horizon.

Nobody looks up when they spill out. The anchor tattoo is a dark oval above a cuff—forearm first, man attached after. The other one's neat in the way men get neat when they want to be invisible. If it's Hale, the name lives in the throat and won't risk the mouth.

No talk at first. Just choreography. One knock, another, one long—metal on metal—like a shared joke that doesn't have to be funny. A box changes hands; not heavy, just careful. That's how you carry names: palms flat, corners level, like guilt might spill. The sea wall counts the seconds between gestures and decides not to remember. If the concrete talked, it would talk in first names and boot sizes.

We don't film. We don't flash. Phones are small traitors. I use a wax pencil to write the rear plate backwards on my knee where light won't find it: KX06… the last two smudged with grit. Goldie clocks the tyres the way some people read palms. "Nearside rear's retread," she whispers. "Chunk missing. Chalk it." She leans out just enough to brush a tiny tick on the rubber with a carpenter's crayon. The wind takes the smell of it and loses interest.

They talk finally; not much. The van door is kind to us and bounces a word back when it shouldn't.

"…Unit Four," says the neat one—too fast, like he tripped on the syllable and pretended it was a step. "Dry dock. Friday. After bells."

"Code stays," anchor says. "Don't look up."

A patrol car decides to be relevant. Its light bar paints the road in soft blues as it creeps past. It hesitates the way teachers do when the bad kid's finally quiet—lingers, judges, moves on. We become furniture. Goldie exhales through her nose, steady and thin; Trixie lowers her chin the way she does on stage when she wants the silence to do the heavy lifting. The patrol car doesn't stop. Rooms take sides; roads pretend they don't. Anchor finishes a smoke he didn't light in front of us. The neat one pockets air like he's short on it. A woman leans half into view at the passenger seat and sparks a lighter; the flame shows a slice of face and the idea of lipstick. Decoration doesn't inhale that carefully. She's either in it, or under it. Trixie's hand rests on the dash like a promise not to move.

"Enough," she says, just breath. "Leave it clean."

We do. The van's taillights don't bother; the gearbox speaks for them. It goes without speaking; the silence does the talking. We let them reach the bend past the sea wall before I start the engine—slow, old, trustworthy—and drop in behind far enough to make doubt our passenger. The train gifts us two notes at the crossing and we pay attention to who flinches. No one does. They've rehearsed not to.

At the roundabout we choose not to be curious. Curiosity is for later. We pass under the street where the lamps have decided to flicker and keep going like it was our plan all along. The lay-by shrinks behind us until it's only a smudge of sodium and sea spray.

"Unit Four," Goldie says into the heater's rattle, filing it under *things we're going to test.* "Dry dock. After bells."

"Keep the names soft," Trixie says. "They'll harden when they need to."

I look at the wax on my knee and the retread tick and think of all the ways a room can turn against you when there aren't any walls. Some debts don't need ceilings to collect; some don't even need names.

"Watch," Trixie says, one more time so the night doesn't forget. "Listen. Leave."

We do.

Chapter 12 — Unit 4, Dry Dock

The bell gives its last tired note and the dock exhales. After bells is when men pretend to forget what they were doing and rooms remember. Unit 4 is a steel chapel—gantries for rafters, chain for hymnals, a floor that learned to hold ships and secrets without complaint. Compressors breathe like patient animals. Sodium lights don't reach the corners; they just suggest them.

We go in with the shift. Hard hats out, heads down, the way water slips into water. The van is already there, backed to the lip, our chalk tick still alive on the nearside rear like a small truth that survived the wash.

Up the side ladder. Hands on rust; boots on rungs with manners. The catwalk gives us the room as a diagram: men as pins, light as string. Down below, anchor-tattoo leans his forearms on the door like he's guarding an idea. The neat one holds a clipboard like it owes him rent. Between them, a third figure never looks up. Some men keep their faces for counting, not for meeting.

"Not heavy," Goldie whispers, clocking the box they pass. "Just careful."

"That's how you carry names," I say, too quiet to travel. "Palms flat, corners level—like guilt might spill."

They don't speak much. They don't need to. The room does half the talking when you teach it how.

"Gate Three. Midnight. Code stays," the neat one says, bored enough to be dangerous. "Three names. Don't look up." He ticks the clipboard with a pencil that's been bitten down to motive.

The compressor chooses that moment to roll its shoulders. Rooms turn on you. They do it without shame; they don't mind who pays. We lose a line to the churn and get it back only as rhythm.

Someone's flashlight climbs the ribbing like a thought you don't want. I file the shape for later; suspicion climbs the same way when it finds a spine. It reaches the catwalk, decides we're shadow, moves on. On the floor, a woman leans out of the van's passenger side and sparks a lighter. Half a face, the idea of lipstick. Decoration doesn't inhale that carefully. She's either in it, or under it.

A worker in a high-vis step into our aisle and starts to look up because that's what people do when the air feels populated. Rooms teach necks where to aim; most nights it's up, some nights it's away.

"Careful on your left, love," Trixie says, just above the compressors, just below trouble. Not a stage voice. A human one. He shifts aside like the room told him to and never knows why.

"Gate Three," Goldie mouths, and taps the metal once with a fingernail like she's setting a metronome only we can hear.

Below, anchor finishes a smoke he never lit in front of anyone. The clipboard goes under an arm. The box travels from door to van with choreography that suggests practice and alibis. The third man—never looking up—stands the way receipts stand up in drawers.

We give the room back to itself. Ladder. Rungs. Air. Out under the arc-light that pretends to be a moon and does a worse job at it.

Past the gate we don't take, the train throws two notes that get swallowed by steel before we can guess the third. If there's a punchline, the dock keeps it for later.

"Walk," Trixie says. "Don't run." The mantra shifts when it needs to. We let it.

On the curb, the van's taillights still can't be bothered; the gearbox does the talking. It goes without speaking. We do the same.

"Gate Three. Midnight," Goldie says to the rattle of a chain that's learned to keep confidence. "Code stays."

"Some debts don't need ceilings to collect," I say, mostly to the steel. "This one's already counting."

We leave the room to choose its side again without us. Out under the real night, the wind remembers its job and spends our heat like small change. Watch. Listen. Leave.

We do.

Chapter 13 — Gate 3, Midnight

Midnight at Gate 3 looks tired of being a noun. The stencil's half a word now—GAT—then rust finishes the sentence. The bell above it has nothing left to say. Arc-lights lay coins of sodium on the concrete and forget to pick them up again. The wind brings salt and diesel and the promise of a dog that never quite barks.

We take the long edge of the fence where the chain link throws a net on the ground. Trixie chooses the sightline that makes the yard think we don't exist. Goldie checks the hinge grease with a fingertip and reads it like tea leaves.

The van arrives with the same dent and the same chalk tick on the nearside rear. Continuity, like a lie that remembered to dress the same. No front plates. Mirrors angled down—men who've been taught not to look up turn glass into pavement.

A yard man does the clipboard dance at the shack. The neat one stands where pencils stand. Anchor leans his forearms on the idea of a door.

We don't film. Phones are little Judas goats. I keep the wax pencil and the notebook and the habit of listening for the thing a room doesn't mean to say.

Trixie gives us three seconds the way she always does—by talking to air that thinks it knows her. "Careful by your boot there, love," she says, soft enough to sound like the night said it. The yard man looks down exactly where she put his attention, and in that small generosity we learn the cadence we came for.

"Monday, then, same code till Monday," the neat one says, bored enough to be dangerous. "Gate Two if weather's wrong." He bites the pencil; the clipboard bites back.

Goldie taps the fence post with a knuckle—one, two—metronome for memory. I grease the inside face of the latch with a smear so mean only a thumbprint will find it. Tiny tail. Harmless to the world, useful to us.

The passenger woman leans far enough into view that the arc-light tries on her cheekbone. Decoration doesn't inhale that carefully. She's either in it, or under it. She doesn't look up. None of them do. Habit is a leash they paid for.

The compressor inside the yard takes a breath and decides not to start. Rooms take sides. This one yawns and ignores us.

"Gate Two if weather's wrong," I whisper it into the paper like a parish clerk writing names that don't belong to him.

We leave before the van decides to be curious. The gearbox does the talking. It goes without speaking; the silence does the talking.

Out by the road, a train throws two notes at the dark and keeps the third because it can. Tonight, it sounds like a calendar being amended.

"Watch," Trixie says, counting us back into the world. "Listen. Leave."

We do.

SC13.5 — Phone (Nightmares — Stinger)

The phone rings like it owes someone an apology. I let it get to three.

A man who doesn't introduce himself: "Small place, small days—wake, smile, sleep, repeat. I'm the change in the pattern. I bring the nightmares."

He waits, like he wants credit.

"Join the queue," I say, and put the receiver down gentle, like a lid on something that might still breathe.

Chapter 14 — Gate 2, Weather's Wrong

The weather keeps its promise. Gate Two sits cleaner than Three—fresh stencil, fresher lies. Drizzle turns the spur road into a mirror that doesn't like what it sees. Arc-lights hang halos over puddles and forget to bless anything. Somewhere inside the yard, a chain drags once and a dog gives a single bark, the kind that sounds like it already knows the answer. Then silence. The kind that chooses sides.

A security bike draws lazy figure-eights, the hub ticking like a bomb that can't find the hour. The dog lifts its head, decides the maths of us isn't worth the bark, and puts it down again. We take the blind corner where the fence doubles itself in water. Goldie watches puddles instead of people; reflections gossip sooner.

The van comes ordinary: same dent, chalk tick half-washed but stubborn. No front plates. Mirrors down. Old habits wearing new wet.

The neat one holds a clipboard under his coat, as if paper can stay dry on a night like this. Anchor does door-leaning like a profession. The passenger woman is only profile and a lighter that won't; she pockets the attempt before the flame gets ideas. They start an exchange and stop it part-way, like someone coughed in the wrong key. A chain somewhere answers with a single cold clink, like punctuation.

"Monday stands. Gate Two only when rain carries," the neat one says. He speaks it to the clipboard first, then the air.

The cyclist rolls toward our corner because curiosity is a wheel with no brake. The dog stands, counts our silhouettes, and decides not to report. His torch begins its climb up the fence.

"Mind your back tyre, love," Trixie says to the rain, same place we hide our breath. "Glass in the puddle."

He looks down exactly where she puts him and turns the beam toward his luck instead of our faces. He rides a smaller circle and pretends it was his idea.

Below, the van gives us two short knocks, then nothing. A cadence that isn't a code yet, but wants paying later. The box trades hands—not heavy, just careful—then goes back again, careful, not heavy. A rehearsal, or a threat.

I write RAIN CARRIES = SWITCH in pencil that doesn't deserve the job. Goldie taps the fence post once, then once again—the shape of Monday in a smaller week.

We leave before the cyclist decides to be thorough. The gearbox says goodnight on behalf of the van. It goes without speaking; the silence does the talking.

Out past the spur, the train tries two notes and lets the wet steal the third before we can call it a joke. The dog gives us a last huff of air—not trust, not threat; an agreement to forget.

Tonight, the weather owns the room.

"Watch," Trixie says. "Listen. Leave."

We do.

Bridge — Monday Carries

The rain forgets itself by morning. Southend pretends at innocence the way towns do on a Monday—bins straight, shop lights honest. My notebook smells of wet card and graphite apology. Gate Two if weather's wrong. Monday stands.

Goldie taps twice on the table, the shape of a week. Trixie reads the silence like a clock and nods once. No speeches. Watch. Listen. Leave.

We go where the room will have to choose a side.

Chapter 15 — Monday Cadence

Monday wears its clean face. Shops open like promises, pavements in their Sunday best. Gate Two if weather's wrong. Monday stands. We're past listening; today is for counting.

Goldie spreads the week on the table—maps, scrawls, names that don't belong to themselves. Two taps. "Gate Three if dry, Two if rain carries." She circles the handoff strip in red like it bleeds on cue.

Trixie picks her place in the picture, and it picks her back—shadow near the bell housing, voice range without echo. "No hardware," she says, like the rule just woke up again. "We move them with a line, not a noise."

Out the window Southend does its little theatre—bus coughs, gulls heckle, a kid practices a punch on lamplight. The air has that before in it, the one rooms recognise.

We mark the cadence on paper, then on bodies:

- I go early (write, listen, find the room's bad ear).
- Goldie watches hands (clipboard, latch, mirror, pockets).
- Trixie keeps the clock (buys three seconds where we need them).

If rain carries, we slide to Gate Two and call it grace. If it doesn't, we stand at Three and call it faith. Either way, we don't ask for permission.

Dusk presses a thumb on the day. Somewhere past the flats a train throws two notes you can measure a plan against. The third keeps its counsel.

"Watch," Trixie says to the window. "Listen," to the door. "Leave," to us.

We do our shoes and our silence in that order.

Chapter 16 — The Room Chooses (Monday Hand-off)

Gate Three looks like it's been forgiven. Stencil scrubbed by weather, bell mute but proud. The concrete holds yesterday's puddles as shallow mirrors and decides not to use them.

We're early the way you're meant to be. I take the long line along the fence and find the room's bad ear—compressor hum to the left, road to the right, a slice in the middle where words fall through. Goldie clocks the handoff strip with a glance—door shadow, latch clean, mirror angle wrong on the van that hasn't arrived yet.

Trixie keeps the clock.

The van comes in like it belongs to the yard. Same dent. Chalk tick still ghosting the tyre, stubborn as regret. No front plates. Mirrors down. Same men: neat at the clipboard, anchor at the door, and the passenger woman in profile, breathing like she owes someone a quiet.

We don't move first. That's how you get counted.

The neat one says it to the air: "Monday stands." He half-bites the pencil, half-believes the sky. "Same code till Friday." He doesn't look up. None of them do.

Goldie's hand rests on the gate post like she owns the metal. Two taps. Not a signal, just a reminder that we have a language.

Trixie steps out of the shadow and borrows the room. "Careful with your box," she says, gentle as a correction you'd thank someone for later. "Edge is split on the bottom." She doesn't point. She doesn't need to.

Anchor checks anyway. The box lifts—not heavy, just careful. The neat one shifts the clipboard, annoyed at gravity. In the three seconds that opens, we learn everything we came for: two short knocks, then nothing on the van skin before the hand-off; the answer is silence unless rain carries.

"Gate Two if weather's wrong," the neat one says to the pencil. The pencil nods.

The cyclist from last night isn't here. A dog coughs once inside the yard and changes its mind about being useful.

Trixie lets the silence decide it belongs to her. She gives it back like a favour.

The box trades hands in the crease of the doorway. Borrowed names move with it—quiet little lives that don't know they're travelling. The mirror lifts just enough to catch the arc-light and put it down again.

We leave on the gearbox talking and make sure it talks before ours does. Out by the road, the train gives two notes like a receipt. The third stays back to mind the till.

"Watch," Trixie says, not to us but to the concrete that's been keeping score. "Listen." To the gate. "Leave." To the night.

We do.

The box isn't heavy. Not tonight. Weight knows when it's been scheduled.

Chapter 17 — The Half Pint (Debrief)

The room's done pretending to be busy. Glasswasher hums like it's praying. Goldie's got the corner booth, elbows on grout that remembers other elbows. Trixie's boots are on the floor—no hardware, just the kind of silence that does work.

On the table: my notebook, her matches, Goldie's empty glass with two taps ghosting the ring.

"Monday stood," Goldie says. Not a question, not a boast.

"It did," I say. "Two short knocks, then nothing. Answer: silence unless rain carries."

Trixie turns a match between finger and thumb. "He said Friday."

"He did," I say. "Clipboard voice."

"So why," Goldie says, "did the van give us three on the pull-away?"

We let the glasswasher finish its prayer.

"Thought it was the hub on the cyclist last night," I say. "Tonight there was no cyclist."

"Three's not their habit," Trixie says. "Men like that don't invent jazz after payday."

Goldie draws a line in the condensation and stops before it becomes a word. "Could be mechanical."

"Could be," I say. I don't believe me.

Trixie lights the match and kills it without using it. Voice over volume—even with fire. "What did the mirror do?"

"Lifted a fraction, then down," Goldie says. "Enough to catch arc-light and let it go." She shrugs. "Could be habit."

"Could be signal," Trixie says. "Could be nerves. Could be telling the woman in the passenger seat to keep breathing."

We sit with the three like it's a guest who arrived early.

"The knocks," I say. "First two… same spacing as yesterday. The third—"

"Late," Goldie says. "Like it wasn't invited."

Trixie folds the spent match back into the book like a pressed flower. "We assume Monday stands. We assume Gate Two if weather's wrong. We do not assume three."

I write it clean: THIRD NOTE = UNPLANNED / PASSENGER / FAILSAFE. The pencil chews back.

From behind the bar, the landlord coughs in the key of go home. We don't.

Goldie produces a paper tray the colour of greaseproof and truth. Cockles and whelks under vinegar. "Eat," she says. "Think better when Essex talks back."

Trixie grins without showing it. "Some men smell like rollmops," she says. "Tonight smelled like paper and fear."

We file the pieces where we keep our knives. Two notes are still ours; the third decides whether it wants to be.

Trixie stands, pushes the glass into the centre so the ring sits perfect. "We write Tuesday like we mean it," she says. "Same rules. Watch. Listen. Leave."

The glasswasher starts again because prayers repeat when they don't hear an answer.

We go.

Chapter 18 — Tuesday Setup: The Third Note

We treat the third knock like it's a stranger who knows our names.

On the table: the strip map of the yard, my notebook open at MONDAY STANDS, Goldie's biro, Trixie's box of matches like a tiny metronome with a temper. The room smells of lemon and last night.

"Three possibilities," I say. "Passenger fail-safe. Mirror signal. Mechanical ghost."

Goldie taps the biro on each, two taps for the ones she hates. "Passenger," she says. "I don't like a woman being the only thing that makes sense."

Trixie turns a match without striking it. "Good," she says. "Sense gets men lazy."

We build Tuesday on tests, not faith.

Test 1 — Acoustic (me): I take the fence line where the yard's bad ear lives—compressor left, road right, a clean pocket for sound. I'll hold the page and time the spacing: first two knocks like Monday, then if the third comes late again, I want the interval. *If it's variable, it's human.*

Test 2 — Visual (Goldie): She owns the mirror. If the glass lifts a hair before the third, that's signal. If passenger tightens her jaw or steals a breath in the same beat, that's fail-safe. If neither moves, call it rattle and we bin the romance.

Test 3 — Controlled delay (Trixie): She buys us three seconds at the hinge with a line that doesn't insult a man's pride. If the third knock only turns up after she speaks, someone's listening for her voice. If it turns up regardless, it's baked into the pull-away and we stop flattering ourselves.

"No hardware," Trixie says, like she's waking the rule again. "We move them with a line, not a noise."

Outside, Southend coughs up a bus and swallows it again. The light has that before-taste the train respects.

Goldie circles the handoff strip in red so neat it looks like paperwork. "Two short knocks, then nothing," she says. "Answer is silence unless rain carries. But if three's late, it's not cadence—it's fear. Or pride."

"Or someone proving they were there," I say. "Men who want credit like to bang the till."

Trixie smiles without displaying the weapon. "Then let them. We'll decide who gets paid."

She lays the matches in a row: four, then two, then one—cheap calendar of a bad week. "Placement," she says. "I'll take bell-shadow. Goldie takes glass. Silias takes the hole in the air."

"Voice over volume," I say.

She nods. "Always."

We write the timer on the page: I count and breathe on the beats so I can read the spacing later from the smudge. Goldie sketches the mirror angle and the passenger's profile with three lines that work harder than they should.

"One more thing," Goldie says. "If mirror lifts without third, we log that as nerves. If third without mirror, log gearbox. If both, signal. If neither, we admit we're romantic and eat our humble pie."

"Pie and mash," I say. "No romance in it. Only gravy."

Trixie pockets the matches, light as sin. "If they give us Gate Two for weather, we don't argue with the sky," she says. "If not, we stand at Three and let the room pick a side."

The wind bothers the pub sign once, decides against a scene. Somewhere past the flats, the train tries two notes and keeps the third under its tongue.

We don't toast. We count.

"Watch," Trixie tells the window. "Listen," she tells the table. "Leave," she tells us.

We do our shoes and our silence in that order.

Chapter 18.5 — Lola: Terms of Introduction

She finds the quiet on purpose. Door cracked, light thin, the rest of the bar held at arm's length.

"Five minutes," she says, like we've already agreed to it.

Goldie folds her arms but not her mouth. "Two."

Lola tips her chin—call it a nod if you need it to be polite. "You're about to test something you didn't make," she says. "Men who think they built the road forget to look both ways."

Trixie doesn't blink. "Name your five down to two."

Lola sets a match on the sill, unlit. "I'm not here to bless you. I'm here to stop you betting the house on a habit."

"The third knock," I say.

She acknowledges it without giving it the compliment of a name. "If it's human, it's either pride or fear. Pride bangs twice so someone hears; fear waits a beat and bangs once for itself." She looks at the corridor like it's a chalkboard. "You'll know the difference by the breath that comes with it."

"Whose breath?" Goldie says.

"Yours," Lola says. "If you're listening wrong."

Trixie smiles the kind that doesn't travel. "And if we're listening right?"

"Then it's theirs," Lola says. "Passenger more than driver. Mirrors tell the truth by mistake."

Goldie leans off the wall. "And you?"

"I don't bless," Lola says again. "But I don't waste air either." She nudges the unlit match toward Trixie with a fingertip. "Keep the box light even when it's heavy. And if the third comes late—don't answer it. Make them bring it."

She turns to go, then remembers to leave a name behind her.

"Lola," she says. Then she writes it slow with the same mouth: "L. O. L. A." A beat. "You'll work out the rest."

Trixie pockets the match like it was always hers. "We usually do," she says.

When we step back into the bar, the noise tries on innocence and fails. The train, somewhere patient, throws two notes and keeps the third where good names live.

We go count.

Chapter 19 — Tuesday: The Third in the Wild

Gate Three again. Same bell, same rust, same air that thinks we won't notice it choosing sides.

Positions: I take the fence pocket where the yard's bad ear lives. Goldie owns the mirror from a shallow angle—glass, latch, hands. Trixie keeps the clock in bell-shadow.

The van arrives wearing its old sins: same dent; chalk tick stubborn on the nearside rear; no front plates; mirrors down. Neat at the clipboard; anchor at the door; passenger woman in profile, breathing careful.

We don't go first.

The skin of the van gives two short knocks, then nothing. The room holds its breath like it's been taught.

Trixie buys us three seconds with a line soft enough to pass for weather. "Mind your edge there, love." No point, no insult.

I count the gap on the page with my breath so I can read the spacing later.

The mirror lifts a hair and settles. Goldie's finger tightens on nothing. The passenger steals a small breath she pretends is noise.

Then the third comes—late. Not loud. Human.

We do not answer it.

The box rises—not heavy, just careful—and pauses on a hinge of silence. The clipboard pretends it's in charge. Somewhere in the yard a dog decides not to report.

"Monday stands," the neat one murmurs to the pencil. "Friday for finish." His eyes stay where habit keeps them.

Trixie gives the silence back like a favour. Voice over volume. She doesn't bless; she calibrates the air.

Goldie watches the mirror instead of the men. It lifts again—half a breath late—and puts the arc-light down like a guilty coin.

I write it clean: THIRD = LATE / MIRROR = NERVES / PASSENGER = FEAR. If it's pride, it's quiet. Quiet men are expensive.

We leave on the gearbox talking and make sure it speaks before ours does. Tail lights don't bother; the road does the telling.

Out by the flats the train gives two notes you could set a watch by. The third sits out, counting us.

"Watch," Trixie says to the bell. "Listen," to the gate. "Leave," to us.

We do.

Chapter 20 — Tuesday: The Third Note

We treat the third knock like it's a stranger who knows our names.

On the table: the strip map of the yard, my notebook open at MONDAY STANDS, Goldie's biro, Trixie's box of matches like a tiny metronome with a temper. The room smells of lemon and last night.

"Three possibilities," I say. "Passenger fail-safe. Mirror signal. Mechanical ghost."

Goldie taps the biro on each, two taps for the ones she hates. "Passenger," she says. "I don't like a woman being the only thing that makes sense."

Trixie turns a match without striking it. "Good," she says. "Sense gets men lazy."

We build Tuesday on tests, not faith.

Test 1 — Acoustic (me): I take the fence line where the yard's bad ear lives — compressor left, road right, a clean pocket for sound. I'll hold the page and time the spacing: first two knocks like Monday, then if the third comes late again, I want the interval. *If it's variable, it's human.*

Test 2 — Visual (Goldie): She owns the mirror. If the glass lifts a hair before the third, that's signal. If passenger tightens her jaw or steals a breath in the same beat, that's fail-safe. If neither moves, call it rattle and we bin the romance.

Test 3 — Controlled delay (Trixie): She buys us three seconds at the hinge with a line that doesn't insult a man's pride. If the third knock only turns up after she speaks, someone's listening for her voice. If it turns up regardless, it's baked into the pull-away and we stop flattering ourselves.

"No hardware," Trixie says, waking the rule again. "Voice over volume. We move them with a line, not a noise."

Outside, Southend coughs up a bus and swallows it again. The light has that before-taste the train respects.

Goldie circles the handoff strip in red so neat it looks like paperwork. "Two short knocks, then nothing," she says. "Answer is silence unless rain carries. But if three's late, it's not cadence — it's fear. Or pride."

"Or someone proving they were there," I say. "Men who want credit like to bang the till."

Trixie smiles without displaying the weapon. "Then let them. We'll decide who gets paid."

She lays the matches in a row: four, then two, then one — cheap calendar of a bad week. "Placement," she says. "I'll take bell-shadow. Goldie takes glass. Silias takes the hole in the air."

"Voice over volume," I say.

She nods. "Always."

We write the timer on the page: I count and breathe on the beats so I can read the spacing later from the smudge. Goldie sketches the mirror angle and the passenger's profile with three lines that work harder than they should.

"One more thing," Goldie says. "If mirror lifts without third, we log that as nerves. If third without mirror, log gearbox. If both, signal. If neither, we admit we're romantic and eat our humble pie."

"Pie and mash," I say. "No romance in it. Only gravy."

Trixie pockets the matches, light as sin. "If they give us Gate Two for weather, we don't argue with the sky," she says. "If not, we stand at Three and let the room pick a side."

The wind bothers the pub sign once, decides against a scene.

Lola: Terms of Introduction

She finds the quiet on purpose. Side corridor. Door cracked, light thin, the rest of the bar held at arm's length.

"Five minutes," she says, like we've already agreed to it.

Goldie folds her arms but not her mouth. "Two."

Lola tips her chin — call it a nod if you need it to be polite. "You're about to test something you didn't make," she says. "Men who think they built the road forget to look both ways."

Trixie doesn't blink. "Name your five down to two."

Lola sets a match on the sill, unlit. "I'm not here to bless you. I'm here to stop you betting the house on a habit."

"The third knock," I say.

She acknowledges it without giving it the compliment of a name. "If it's human, it's either pride or fear. Pride bangs twice so someone hears; fear waits a beat and bangs once for itself." She looks at the corridor like it's a chalkboard. "You'll know the difference by the breath that comes with it."

"Whose breath?" Goldie says.

"Yours," Lola says. "If you're listening wrong."

"And if we're listening right?" Trixie asks.

"Then it's theirs," Lola says. "Passenger more than driver. Mirrors tell the truth by mistake." She nudges the unlit match toward Trixie. "Keep the box light even when it's heavy. And if the third comes late — don't answer it. Make them bring it."

She turns to go, then remembers to leave a name behind her.

"Lola," she says. Then she writes it slow with the same mouth: "L. O. L. A." A beat. "You'll work out the rest."

Trixie pockets the match like it was always hers. "We usually do," she says.

When we step back into the bar, the noise tries on innocence and fails. Somewhere patient, the train throws two notes and keeps the third where good names live.

Gate Three

Evening dry enough to lie about it; the yard tastes of wet rope and Monday's echo.

Positions: I take the fence pocket where the yard's bad ear lives. Goldie owns the mirror from a shallow angle — glass, latch, hands. Trixie keeps the clock in bell-shadow.

The van arrives wearing its old sins: same dent; chalk tick stubborn on the nearside rear; no front plates; mirrors down. Neat at the clipboard; anchor at the door; passenger woman in profile, breathing careful.

We don't go first.

The skin of the van gives two short knocks, then nothing. The room holds its breath like it's been taught.

Trixie buys us three seconds with a line soft enough to pass for weather. "Mind your edge there, love." No point, no insult.

I count the gap on the page with my breath so I can read the spacing later.

The mirror lifts a hair and settles. Goldie's finger tightens on nothing. The passenger steals a small breath she pretends is noise.

Then the third comes — late. Not loud. Human. We do not answer it.

The box rises — not heavy, just careful — and pauses on a hinge of silence. The clipboard pretends it's in charge. Somewhere in the yard a dog decides not to report.

"Monday stands," the neat one murmurs to the pencil. "Friday for finish." His eyes stay where habit keeps them.

Trixie gives the silence back like a favour. Voice over volume. She doesn't bless; she calibrates the air.

Goldie watches the mirror instead of the men. It lifts again — half a breath late — and puts the arc-light down like a guilty coin.

I write it clean: THIRD = LATE / MIRROR = NERVES / PASSENGER = FEAR. If it's pride, it's quiet. Quiet men are expensive.

We leave on the gearbox talking and make sure it speaks before ours does. Tail lights don't bother; the road does the telling. Out by the flats the train gives two notes you could set a watch by. The third sits out, counting us.

"Watch," Trixie says to the bell. "Listen," to the gate. "Leave," to us.

We do.

The Cost of Quiet

The Half Pint is half-cleaned; jukebox dark; landlord polishing the same glass like it owes him rent. The room is done talking. What's left is the bill.

Goldie owns the corner booth again — two rings ghosting the varnish where her glass used to live. She gives the table two taps; the wood remembers her anyway.

"Late third," she says. "Mirror twitched. Passenger breathed."

"Quiet men are expensive," I say. "Loud ones just send the invoice."

Trixie sets her matchbox metronome down and doesn't open it. "We don't pay in panic. We pay in placement. Tomorrow we don't correct them. We let them correct themselves."

On the tray: pie and mash, steam like a sermon. Cockles and whelks sweating vinegar beside it because Essex insists. The smell makes honesty feel heavier.

Goldie forks the pie like it might confess. "If they're counting us," she says, "they'll try to make three sound like home."

"We don't live there," Trixie says. "No hardware. Voice over volume. We keep the room. They can have the noise."

I write it clean so tomorrow can read it:

- THIRD = keep unacknowledged (no reward).
- MIRROR = watch jaw, not glass.
- PASSENGER = fear tells the truth once.

The landlord coughs in the key of go home. We don't. Outside, the train gives two notes as if to remind the street how to breathe. The third sits it out with the smokers.

Trixie closes the matchbox and the room goes with it. "We're not brave," she says. "We're careful. Let the brave boys bang the tin."

We let the pie cool the way decisions do. Then we go.

Chapter 21 — Borrowed Names

Names don't weigh much until they're in the wrong place.

Goldie lays the handoff list — a smear-stamped photocopy that smells of toner and the kind of office that never opens a window. She's got three columns straight as a sermon: who, when, where. The who is where the teeth are.

"Here," she says, tapping a line that learned to lie. "H. Vale yesterday. H. Vale again today. Same hand, same loop on the H, same lazy tail on the e."

"And?" I say, though the room already told me.

She slides my notebook across so Monday STANDS can look Tuesday in the eye. "Different van," she says. "Same dent, same chalk tick, no front plates — but the registration the clip-voice read at the gate doesn't match the number typed on Vale's line."

Trixie doesn't blink. "Men who like third knocks also like borrowing plates. And names."

Goldie peels the corner back. There's a sticker under the photocopy — wholesaler logo selling biscuits no one buys in places like this. Sweetness pretending. "It's not just plates," she says. "It's paperwork."

I write it so simple it can't pretend: H. VALE = REAL / ENTRY = COPIED WRONG ON PURPOSE / VAN = BORROWED NAME.

"Do we fix it?" Goldie asks. She already knows the answer.

"We don't fix their story," Trixie says. "We write ours on top and leave theirs underneath where it itches."

"What about Friday?" I say. The word tastes like a door we're going to have to use.

Trixie looks past us, through the glass, into a street that hasn't chosen a side yet. "Friday's for men who believe in endings," she says. "We believe in exits."

The photocopier glow dies. Outside, somebody tries a laugh and gets a cough. In the distance the train throws two notes and keeps the third for whoever needs reminding.

Goldie draws a small cross next to H. Vale — not a prayer, a pin. "We let him be real," she says. "We let the van be wrong."

Trixie pockets the list like a promise. "Tomorrow we ask for nothing and learn twice as much. Watch. Listen. Leave."

We leave the table the way you leave a sleeping dog that might wake helpful.

Chapter 22 — Borrowed Time, Borrowed Names

Southend does a good impression of ordinary when it wants to. Monday afternoon keeps its head down; shutters rattle like they've been told off and learned from it. The pie-and-mash by the station smells of pepper and yesterday's steam—the sort of place that files secrets under "gravy" and never checks the drawer again.

We take the corner booth that's tried to retire three times and been talked out of it by bleach. Goldie sits sideways to the door, which is her version of manners. Trixie keeps her hands wrapped round a tea she won't finish. Lola watches the window the way a tailor watches cloth: measuring, not admiring.

"Same van'll try again," I say. "No plates front. Box rides careful. Different driver if they're bright."

Trixie nods once. That's all the speech we're allowed before the week makes up its mind.

A kid in hi-vis comes in for three eels and a joke he never tells. The air does that thing where it chooses who it belongs to. Today it doesn't pick us, but it knows our names.

"Your turn," Goldie says, chin at me. "If we're the band, you carry the cases."

"I handle the cases," I say. "Different religion."

The woman behind the counter calls me "love" like it's a loan. I pay for two and ask for one bag—sharing earns trust in places like this. She slides over a paper parcel warm enough to explain loyalty. The greaseproof peeks like a tongue that knows better than to speak.

Outside, the weather can't remember what it promised. Clouds stack like unpaid bills and move on with a shrug. Down on the forecourt, the train pushes two notes into the afternoon and swallows the third. Private joke again. If there's a punchline, it doesn't think we've earned it.

"Where?" Trixie asks.

"Lay-by past the lights," I say. "Where the concrete talks in first names and boot sizes."

"Good," she says. "I'm tired of full names."

Lola doesn't smile, exactly—she edits her face. "We don't go to the lay-by," she says. "We let the lay-by come to us." There's a flicker there—could be doubt, could be nostalgia—the look people get when a station platform remembers their name before they do.

Goldie flicks her lighter without lighting anything. Signal, not habit. "Heard that."

We take the long way, past the betting shop that owes everybody a Tuesday and the barber that cuts hair like an apology. Trixie slows by the charity window and checks herself in a kettle she doesn't need, then lifts her chin half an inch.

"You look like trouble," Goldie says.

"Good. Saves time."

At the corner we stop because that's where you stop. A patrol car idles across the road with the patience of a teacher who knows the bad kid is trying to be good—for now. It lingers, judges, moves on, proud of itself for not making a scene.

"There," Lola says—no point. She folds the word like paper and tucks it behind our ears. The van eases through the traffic the way lies ease through polite rooms: slow, careful, already forgiven by somebody we haven't met.

No plates front. Tailgate that learned manners but not grammar. It rolls past as if we're furniture and the world is staged for somebody else's monologue.

"That box isn't heavy," I say. "It's careful. That's how you carry names: palms flat, corners level, like guilt might spill."

"Whoever's got it thinks they're alone," Lola says. "They only breathe when the road does."

"Which is why they miss the part where the road holds its breath," Trixie says, and looks at me for the rest.

We don't follow. Rooms turn on you; streets do it without shame. We take the next alley—bins straight, brickwork patched with old anger. The van pauses at the junction the way men do when they're about to make a mistake look intentional. Then it goes left, which is right, and we go right, which is left, and the city applauds us for pretending we didn't see each other.

At the end of the alley a door tries to be unremarkable and fails. It wears a smear of oil like a bruise and smells faintly of vinegar—the cockles have been here, or somebody who loves them has. Trixie presses it with two fingers and the building decides not to mind.

Inside it's dark enough to keep its own diary. Somewhere a compressor coughs and then pretends it didn't. We take in the room without moving much: heater ticking itself into a better mood; a desk that believes in paper; a kettle that doesn't.

Lola tilts her head. "Run it from the kettle," she says to nobody that should exist. "That's where truth forgets itself."

Goldie closes the door with her hip, quiet as regret. Her eyes do a tour—hinges, corners, window latch, our backs. "We're good," she says. "For the next three sentences."

Footsteps outside, then a man talking to a problem like it owes him the last word. He doesn't come in; he edits his route and argues with his cigarette instead. Some people mistake nicotine for strategy.

Trixie breathes once, shallow. "If it opens," she whispers, "we laugh. Like we belong here and the rent's paid."

"And if it doesn't?" I say.

"We'll still laugh," she says. "We'll just charge extra."

The room decides to like us. The heater finds its job. The compressor steadies the way drunks think they do. Lola crosses to the desk and doesn't touch anything; she touches time. There are notes here—smudged pencil weather maps of men who forgot the forecast is always the same: wait, move, take.
A battered archive box sulks under the desk, lid not quite shut—the kind of container that learns your secrets by holding its breath.
Boxes practice loyalty; names teach them betrayal.

She frowns at a stain shaped like an idea that lost the vote. "They rehearse here," she says. "Not words—behaviour."

"That box is rehearsal," I say. "When they think it's light enough, they'll try it on."

"And if it's not?" Goldie asks.

"Then somewhere else gets paid."

The footsteps return, closer now, reconsidering courage. Trixie slides into the chair behind the desk and arranges her mouth into something that could invoice you for smiling. "Go on then," she murmurs to the air. "Make me earn my living."

The handle tries the future, thinks better of it, and retreats. Outside, a dog barks once, then remembers wages aren't worth it.

We don't move for a while. We let the room cash its promise. The light at the window brightens like it found change in its pocket. When we go, we do it the way you leave a sleeping dog who might wake helpful.

Out on the street the train gives us two notes again and keeps the third. Somewhere between the van and the air somebody decides they can afford to wait till tonight. Good. So can we.

Back at the pie-and-mash, the woman behind the counter recognises our silence and prices it fairly. I pass the bag to Trixie. She peels back the paper, breathes pepper and Monday and everything we didn't say.

"Not bad for a girl going nowhere," Goldie says, and steals a fork.

Trixie looks at the window, which looks back like it knows a secret. "I'm already standing," she says. "Let the rest catch up."

"Watch," Lola says, soft as policy. "Listen. Leave."

We do. The shop keeps our heat like small change and spends it on the next faces with the same problem. The train swallows the third note again, not stingy—just saving it for tonight.

Some debts don't need ceilings to collect. Some don't even need names.

Micro-Bridge — Evening Carries

Evening irons the day flat and leaves the creases where we'll need them.
The pie-and-mash greaseproof cools to a quiet promise; boxes practice loyalty, people don't.
Lola says nothing and edits the room instead; whatever she felt at the window has gone to ground.
Goldie palms the lighter once—signal, not spark—then pockets the question she almost asked.
Trixie stands like a verdict that hasn't picked a defendant.
The heater in the office remembers our names badly; the street remembers them better.
The van is somewhere rehearsing its alibi; we rehearse not needing one.
The train tries two notes, swallows the third again—saving it for when somebody finally pays.

Chapter 23 — Gate Two Learns Our Names

Gate Two looks innocent in daylight. By evening it learns better. The fence line hums with bored electricity and a habit of letting the wrong people through if they knock in the right rhythm. Someone's hung a "NO PARKING" sign across a dent shaped like a promise nobody kept.

We post up where the street can't quite make its mind up about being industrial or domestic. Flats with washing lines on one side; a yard with pallets on the other; a fox that doesn't pay council tax trotting through the middle like a landlord. The smell's a mix of diesel, old rope, and last week's rain trying to file an appeal.

"Same van comes back, it'll pick the shadow with the least opinions," I say.

"Trixie's got opinions," Goldie says, and smiles without teeth.

"I've got standards," Trixie says. "Different animal."

Lola hasn't spoken yet. She does that when the world is noisy—trims it down, edits it into something she can live with. She watches the gate like she's reading a page that wants to smudge itself. When a kettle starts up somewhere deep in the yard, she nods the way snipers nod at wind.

"Truth forgets itself at the kettle," she says, almost to the fence. "Same as yesterday. If they confess, it'll be in steam."

We work quiet. Goldie counts footsteps between the road and the gate—eight on the left, nine on the right if you're lazy. Trixie rehearses nothing; she just stands where the light can't find her and lets the light apologise. I track lines of sight and lies of habit: who glances up the road, who never does; which window cares; which doesn't.

A train gives us two notes and holds back the third. The joke's older now. It knew our names yesterday; today it's decided to learn the spellings.

"Timing?" Goldie asks.

"When they think we've gone home," I say. "When the compressor's cooled and the radio's bored of itself."

"Good," Trixie says. "Then we won't have to pretend we like their music."

The first rehearsal is never the show. We get a rusted Transit with a bumper held on by faith, a kid in a tabard whose shoulders learned to shrug before they learned to carry, a woman in a puffa jacket talking into her phone like it owes her rent. All wrong shapes. All wrong pace.

Gate Two yawns and lets them through anyway. Gates are like pubs—they don't judge, they just tally.

Lola finally speaks. "When they come, it'll be careful," she says. "Careful is louder than fast."

She's right. When trouble's proud of itself, it sprints. When it's scared of names, it tiptoes.

We take it in shifts to look like we're not looking. Goldie buys three teabags at the corner shop and pays in shrapnel. Trixie pretends to be a woman waiting for a bus that hasn't believed in buses for years. I take a walk that maps the drains: where water decides to leave, where it reconsiders.

By the bins outside the tyre place I find a cardboard box with the corners reinforced in brown tape, lid soft from being opened too many times. Not *the* box; a cousin. The world's full of cousins. I tilt it with my boot. It smells of rubber dust and something like peppermint, the cheap kind that tries too hard.

"Practice," I say, when I'm back. "Somebody's been rehearsing their hands."

"Hands always tell on people," Trixie says. "It's the rest of them that learns stagecraft."

A light comes on in the yard office, then off again. Someone's remembered something; someone's forgotten something else. Lola tilts her head a second time. "Two inside," she says. "One new, one who teaches."

"How do you know?" Goldie asks.

"They started the kettle twice," Lola says. "That's how you welcome someone and pretend you didn't."

We give it another twenty minutes because patience pays better than pride. The street decides to share itself out—fox to the hedge, wind to the fence, a patrol car to the far end where it can feel useful without doing anything reckless.

When the van finally shows, it doesn't commit at first. Rolls past once. Thinks better of the thinking-better. Comes back slower, finding love notes in potholes where none exist. No plates on the front. A tailgate that's learned how to apologise in three languages without meaning it. Careful, like Lola said—careful enough to be loud.

Trixie doesn't move. She narrows a thought and the air makes room for it. If the driver looked her way, he'd feel it—a pressure change with a lipstick line.

"Which way when they leave?" Goldie asks.

"Left," I say. "They'll want the river in their mirrors. Makes men think the evidence will float away."

"Left is right," Goldie says. We've been here before.

The gate blinks awake. A man steps out to meet the van, wearing a smile that doesn't belong to him, like he's borrowed it from someone braver and forgotten to return it. He taps the bonnet twice—polite as a knock on a coffin. The van inches forward; the gate decides it's had enough principles for one evening and slides aside.

We don't go in. That's not tonight's job. Tonight's job is to learn their rhythm and decide where to stand when the song repeats.

"Count," Trixie whispers.

I count. One, two, three—pause. Four. The sound of a box being lifted by someone who thinks weight is the same as guilt. It's not. Guilt is the slosh when you carry it wrong.

The lid gives the smallest chirp—then flinches, like it heard itself. Boxes practice loyalty; sooner or later, even cardboard learns to doubt its handlers.

Goldie's hands stay loose. "If the lid chirps, we're early," she says. "If it sulks, we're late."

"It's learning to sulk," Lola says. "Same lesson as yesterday."

Movement at the office window: a woman's silhouette, slice of face, the idea of lipstick. Decoration doesn't inhale that carefully. She's either in it, or under it. She watches the box for a second too long and then remembers to be scenery.

A dog barks from somewhere behind the pallets and regrets the decision immediately. The man with the borrowed smile laughs for show; the driver doesn't. He's saving all his shows for later. He carries the box like we said—palms flat, corners level, truth trying not to spill—and the new lock on the office door pretends it was always there.

They don't stay long. People rarely do when they know their own names are arguing with the room. The box disappears, returns wearing the same lid but a different story. The borrowed smile thanks the driver for a service nobody paid for out loud. The gate gives a small shrug and the van rolls back to the street like it's learned grace.

We don't follow. We drift. Left, as predicted, which is right. The van chooses the slowest part of the road on purpose—a man's idea of subtlety. The patrol car finds something else to be patient about. The fox resumes its tax-free trot.

"Later," Trixie says. "We take the long way and arrive before they do."

"Pie and mash first?" Goldie says, because it's habit to make the world ordinary before you make it complicated.

Trixie shakes her head. "Later," she says again, softer now. Not a refusal—a rhythm. The kind of word people use when they trust themselves not to hurry.

We cut through a run of terraces where every window holds a different decision: net curtains, no curtains, plants that needed you to come home sooner. A man on a step fixes a bicycle he doesn't want to ride. A woman drags a bin like it insulted her mother. Life, rehearsing itself.

By the time we reach the street that pretends not to connect to Gate Two, the van has made the mistake of believing its own timing. It pulls in half a length from a lay-by that remembers more names than it should. The driver gets out and does the stretch all liars do: hands on hips, spine popping, dignity borrowed, like the smile.

We don't look at him. We look at the daylight that's nearly done with us and the first window lights that think they're not witnesses. Lola's voice stays small. "He'll check his phone, then the mirror, then the phone again. Third one is fear."

"Fear makes men noisy," Trixie says, not unkind. "I prefer quiet."

He does it like she said: phone, mirror, phone. Then he opens the back and talks to the box with his hands. It answers by hesitating—just a flicker—and then behaving. Loyalty first. Betrayal only when you earn it.

Goldie shifts her weight and the pavement forgives her. "What's the play?" she says.

"Nothing noisy," I say. "We keep the rhythm. We learn the hinge and the habit. We make them want to repeat themselves."

"Then we interrupt the repetition," Trixie says, and finally smiles. Not the smile you invoice for—the other one. The one that makes weather remember its manners.

The driver closes the doors badly and doesn't notice. The third note arrives from the rails and calls his bluff. He hears it. He doesn't know he's heard it. He gets back in and leaves like silence gets paid overtime.

We let the street breathe. We count to the number the gate used. We count to the number the box taught its lid. We don't follow. Not tonight.

"Tomorrow," Goldie says.

"Tonight," Lola says. "When the kettle tells on them."

Trixie looks at both of them and then past them, to where the river finishes other people's sentences. "This is where it starts," she says. "Where names wash thin and truths decide whether to float."

She turns for home without turning her back on anything. We move with her because that's the work—keep the centre where you can see it, and teach the edges to behave.

Behind us, Gate Two forgets what it learned and starts again.

The train tries two notes and keeps the third—saving it for when somebody finally pays, or when we do.

Either way, it's coming.

Micro-Bridge — The City Lowers Its Voice

Night puts felt on its shoes.
Southend swaps neon for advice and forgets both by midnight.
The notebook opens where steam once spoke; the page remembers the words better than the mouths did.
We go back to the room that tried to like us.

Chapter 24 — The Kettle Tells On Them

The office wears dark like a decent suit—pressed, practical, pretending it wasn't bought on tick. We slip in on the hinge's second thought. The heater coughs once and decides to behave; the compressor keeps time like it owes us a favour.

"Same chairs," Goldie says, touching nothing. "Different story."

"Stories don't change," Trixie says. "People do."

Lola goes to the counter and lays two fingers on the kettle as if it were a wrist. "Warm," she says. "Not recent. Truth cooled before we got here."

"Their kind of religion," I say. "Confession, then tea."

We move the way you read a room you've already met—slower, kinder, sterner. Notes on the desk: smudged pencil weather again, isobars of intention. A line that started confident and finished as a shrug. Somebody rehearsed a delivery and lost nerve at the verb.

Under the desk, the archive box acts normal on purpose. Lid squared, tape clean, corners tight with good behaviour. It's the kind of obedience that learns from being watched.

"Lid'll chirp if it thinks no one's listening," Goldie says.

"Then we listen like furniture," Trixie says, and sits in the boss's chair without asking its feelings.

I take the room's temperature the old way: blinds for fingerprints, waste bin for timelines, kettle for guilt. On the corkboard, a calendar from two months ago insists on the present; a Post-it says "PLATES?" with a question mark that knows the answer.

Footsteps pass the window—one set, not hurried. The handle wonders about the future, chooses not to open it. A dog edits its bark down to a cough.

"Tomorrow," Lola says to the kettle, not to us. "You'll forget again."

She tilts the lid a breath. The box hesitates—nothing dramatic, just the flinch cardboard does when it thinks a name is about to be said out loud. Loyalty first. But even loyalty hates embarrassment.

"That's our gap," I say. "Embarrassment's where truth trips."

Trixie nods once. "We'll make them repeat themselves until the room's bored of their version."

Goldie gestures at the window latch. "If we're coming back, we don't break anything. We just teach the air to remember us."

"Leave cleaner than we found," I say.

"Except the silence," Trixie says. "We muss that up."

I kneel, palms flat, and slide the box an inch, just enough to hear the scrape it makes when it pretends it's never moved. It's heavier in the way paperwork is heavy: weightless until the bill arrives.

"Two names inside," Lola says, eyes shut like she's reading braille off the steam. "One that wants to be called something else."

Goldie smiles without showing it. "Borrowed, then."

"Borrowed," Lola agrees. "And due back soon."

Outside, the train gives two notes and withholds the third—same private joke, closer to the punchline. The river smell threads in through the gap in the frame, finishing other people's sentences in brine.

Trixie stands. The chair forgives her quickly. "We don't take," she says. "We invite. Make the box want to tell on itself."

"How?" Goldie asks.

"Make the room feel safe," Trixie says. "Then make the men feel clever. Clever men always talk."

We leave in the order the carpet will approve of later: me first, Goldie on hinges, Lola on weather, Trixie last, because verdicts don't rush. The door closes like it's been taught, and the lock remembers its manners.

At the yard edge, night pretends it's new here. Gate Two breathes out and in, content with its shift work. Across the way, the river glints like a good liar—honest about being a surface, truthful about hiding depth.

"Tomorrow," I say, out of habit.

"Tonight," Lola answers, out of faith. "When the kettle warms."

Trixie half-smiles, the one the weather obeys. "We'll let the box doubt itself a little longer. Doubt's heavy. Men hate carrying it."

The third note finally lands—late, deliberate, earned. It sounds like a door we'll open when the room chooses us back.

We walk, and the street keeps our heat for whoever needs courage after we're gone.

Micro-Bridge — Steam Remembers

We take the long way so the street can forget our footprints.
By the time we reach the yard, the night has ironed out its creases and left one on purpose.
Somewhere behind the blinds, a kettle decides what kind of noise to make.

Chapter 26 — When the Kettle Decides

The office meets us halfway—door gives easy, light goes up slow, heater clears its throat like it's been thinking about us. The compressor starts a sentence and leaves it mid-air.

Then the kettle goes off like a confession that overshot the mark—one clean, high whistle that slices the dark—then silence, sudden, deliberate. Not empty; chosen.

Goldie closes the door with her hip. "That's a warning," she says.

"That's a welcome," Trixie says, and puts two fingers on the counter like checking a pulse. "Rooms say hello how they like."

Lola listens the way tailors watch cloth: measuring, not admiring. "It wanted to speak," she says. "Then it remembered consequences."

The archive box sits where we left it, squared to the skirting, obedient as alibis. The lid has learned manners; the tape pretends it's always been tidy.

"We touch it, we teach it," I say. "We don't touch it, it teaches us."

Trixie nods to the desk chair and the chair forgives us in advance. "Palms flat. Corners level. Like guilt might spill."

We lift the lid a thumb's width—enough air to count as trust, not enough to count as theft. The box flinches. Cardboard learns from people.

Inside: a cassette in a clear case, a roll of blank adhesive labels, a thick black marker breathing solvent into the dark. The tape's spine bears a name—written, crossed out, another name written over it, half-peeled as if the truth got itchy and tried to climb out.

Inside isn't evidence—it's a decision. A name that was never meant to be written, waiting to see who says it out loud.

Goldie whistles low without music. "Borrowed," she says. "Due back with new handwriting."

"Not contents," Lola says softly. "Instruction."

Trixie takes the pen, tests the cap, doesn't open it. She looks at the crossed-out name like it owes her rent. "They're not moving truth," she says. "They're renaming it."

I check the room for audience: blinds learning our fingerprints, heater remembering our heat badly, the calendar still insisting on the present tense. On the corkboard, a Post-it in the same blocky hand: **PLATES?** The question mark knows the answer and pretends not to. In the waste bin: an envelope with **POSTAGE?**—same hand, same doubt.

"Same writer," I say. "Practises lies in print so the cursive won't testify."

Lola closes her eyes. "The passenger," she says, almost to steam. "She saw herself in us. She'll start editing mirrors next."

"Good," Trixie says. "Mirrors are lazy witnesses."

We don't press play. We don't rename anything. We let the box sit with its choices the way you let a man sit with his story until it stops flattering him.

"What's the move?" Goldie asks.

"Make them repeat themselves," Trixie says. "Then make them hear it."

"How?"

Trixie sets the pen down, deliberate as a verdict. "We put the label back flat and leave it blank. Blank is heavier than ink. Clever men always talk; blank space shames them into paragraphs."

The kettle clicks alive again—no whistle this time, just the steady, private boil of someone deciding whether to tell the whole thing or the useful part.

"Tea?" I say.

"Hospitality," Trixie says. "We'll need it. When the room chooses us back, it'll want to be fed."

Lola reaches into the box and doesn't take the tape; she smooths the peeled label down with a fingertip, gentle as fixing a collar. "Names don't like second chances," she says. "Let's give them one anyway."

We close the lid—palms flat, corners level. The box behaves, which is suspicious. Outside, the rails spend two notes and save the third like a tip for good service.

"Tomorrow," Goldie says.

"Tonight," Trixie answers. "When someone realises blank is an accusation."

We leave the way we came in—evidence of nothing, scent of steam. The door settles. The lock remembers our names well enough to miss us.

On the forecourt, a passing car window holds the passenger's face for half a second and then lets it go. If she comes back, she'll come without lipstick or with too much. That's how reflections argue.

The river finishes someone else's sentence in brine. The third note doesn't arrive, and that's the message.

"Boxes practice loyalty," I say.

"People don't," Trixie says. "Which is how we win."

Lola listens to the night until it edits itself smooth. "Next time," she says, "we let the kettle boil over."

Goldie grins like a match that knows its job. "And charge extra for mopping up."

Micro-Bridge — Blank Is Loud

We leave the label blank on purpose.
By morning, the city has opinions about it.
Truth hates a silence that's shaped like a question.

Chapter 27 — The Label Shames Them

Monday turns the dimmer up but won't commit to daylight. Southend does its usual impression of respectable: bins neat, shutters cooperative, the lie of order tidied to the kerb.

We split like we mean to meet later even if we don't. Goldie walks a half-step ahead, jangling change like she's negotiating with luck. Lola keeps time with the river—two notes of the rails spent, the third tucked away like a secret it isn't ready to explain. Trixie moves last, because verdicts don't hurry and the weather needs someone to copy.

"Same plan," she says. "Let clever talk. We listen like furniture."

The office chooses to remember us. The door unlearns its squeak; the light comes up like a blush that's decided to be useful. The heater tries our names in the wrong order, then gets close enough.

On the desk: yesterday's pencil weather, isobars of intention smudged into doubt. On the corkboard: the calendar still insisting on now, and the familiar blocky hand—**PLATES?** — as if the question mark wants a raise. Below it, a scrap pinned badly: **POSTAGE?** Same capitals, same nervous curve, same man fighting his handwriting for custody of the truth.

Same blocky capitals, same nervous hook on the question mark—as if the pen can't stop asking even when the man won't.

Goldie steps to the window and checks the yard's reflection. "Our friend with the borrowed grin?" she says. "He the type to come back for his pride?"

"Pride travels," I say. "Receipts don't."

Lola tilts her head toward the counter and lays two fingers on the kettle like a pulse. "Warm," she says. "Felt like speaking. Chose not to. They're trying honesty as a costume."

Trixie looks at the archive box the way good teachers look at chairs that swear they weren't scraped. The lid is squared, the tape obedient. The blank label lies there like a mirror with no patience.

"Moment of truth," she says, gentle as a warning. "Or at least of punctuation."

She lifts the lid a breath. The cassette sits where we left it, spine forward, the old name crossed out, the new one attempted—peeled back to blank. Beside it: the thick marker, cap on tight like it's got nothing to confess.

Goldie reaches—stops herself a hair before touching. "Blank's doing the work already."

"Men hate blank," Trixie says. "It's the only silence that interrupts."

The handle tests a future, then chooses drama. The door opens for a man who thinks entering is half the victory. He's yesterday's driver dressed as today's supervisor; the borrowed grin has been ironed, but it still hangs wrong.

He stops when he sees us treating his room like it might deserve better.

"Private premises," he says, as if the words could invoice us.

"Then name the job," Trixie says. "Private things have names. Stolen ones use other people's."

He points at the box without pointing, the way cowards do. "That's ours."

"It's borrowed," I say. "Due back with the truth you promised it."

The kettle clicks, not quite a whistle—more of a throat-clear a priest makes before the bad part. He startles. Proud men always flinch at domestic noises; they know kitchens tell on them.

Lola speaks without raising her voice. "Your label's fallen off," she says—kind as a cut. "You tried the second name and it didn't take."

His eyes go to the marker. He doesn't pick it up. Men rarely accept invitations that require handwriting.

"Admin error," he says.

"Errors don't peel themselves," Goldie says, and lets her lighter click without flame. Signal, not habit. The room notices. Rooms like competence.

He does that laugh men keep for when they want to sound taller. "I don't need to explain myself."

Trixie smiles in a way that edits the weather. "Brilliant," she says. "Save it for when the room asks you again."

He blinks. He doesn't understand. The box does. Cardboard's smarter than pride if you give it time.

Behind him, the passenger hesitates—slice of face at the doorjamb, lipstick downgraded to memory. She catches herself in the window—our faces, her face, the lie—and decides the glass can't help. Mirrors are lazy witnesses. She looks at people instead.

"You don't have to rename it," Lola says, to her, not him. "You can call it by its first name and survive. It will be heavier for a while."

The passenger's hand lifts, then doesn't. A habit you can see from across the room: the reflex to tidy truth until it fits the page. She lowers her hand into her own pocket as if she's remembered where she keeps her bravery.

He tries authority on again. "Let's not make a scene."

"Scenes don't make themselves," Trixie says. "People do. Boxes just keep score."

He steps toward the desk and the blank label blinks at him. That's the thing about blank: it's louder in daylight. He reaches for the pen, stops. Reaches again, stops nearer.

"While you decide," I say, "a question."

He hates questions. "What."

I tap the corkboard. **PLATES?** The nervous hook of the question mark is the same as the one on the **POSTAGE?** envelope in the bin. "You been practising your lies in block capitals because your cursive tells on you?"

Silence arrives to hear its own name said out loud.

Goldie keeps her eyes on the window. "Patrol rolling slow."

The driver looks at the patrol car, at us, at the label blank as judgement. He picks up the pen like it might bite him—cap off, click, hesitation.

"Don't," Trixie says, soft as mercy. "Blank is the truth you can live with."

He hates that sentence. Men with short ladders always do.

The passenger finds a voice that doesn't belong to him. "Leave it," she says, barely above steam. "You can carry weight and still go home."

His jaw tries a new shape. "Whose side are you on?"

"Names," she says. "Mine."

Lola doesn't smile; she edits the air. "Good."

The kettle decides to boil properly, a clean, rising line that sounds like a story getting tired of being handled. He flinches again, smaller this time. Pride's a muscle; you can train it to stop jerking.

"We're done," he says—but he's asking the room, not us.

The room declines to answer. The heater remembers our heat; the blinds remember theirs. That's a draw. Draws embarrass men who need wins.

He recaps the pen with the finality of a man pretending he chose not to speak. The label stays blank. Blank wins.

The marker sits capped like a kept secret. When it's uncapped, somebody's chosen a version of the truth. When it snaps, they've chosen noise.

"We'll be back," he says, but the sentence doesn't believe him.

"Good," Trixie says. "Bring your handwriting."

They leave. The passenger doesn't look at the window. She looks at Trixie and doesn't edit her face. That's a start.

She stops asking glass to tell the truth and starts watching faces instead.

We let the door settle. The compressor finishes its sentence. The kettle drops to the hush that comes after choosing.

The kettle doesn't whistle; it hisses, then thinks better of speaking. That's when people do.

Goldie exhales the shape of a laugh. "Blank is expensive," she says.

"Worth every penny," Trixie answers. "It buys the part where men tell on themselves."

Lola strokes the peeled edge down again, deliberate as smoothing a lapel before a difficult truth. "Next time," she says, "the room will pick a side."

"Rooms always do," I say. "They just pretend they're neutral first."

Outside, the rails spend two notes and save the third for someone who's earned it. The river finishes a sentence no one started and moves on without applause.

We leave cleaner than we came: no prints that matter, no labels that lie, a little less heat for the room to miss.

On the street, Southend tries faith for five seconds and then remembers Monday. The patrol car lingers like a teacher proud of behaving; it moves on when no one misbehaves loudly enough to justify a lesson.

"Tea?" I say, out of habit.

"Pie and mash," Trixie says, out of rule. "Blank tastes better with pepper."

Lola listens to the city choosing its voice. "And after," she says, "we teach the box to speak without names."

Goldie's lighter clicks once—signal received. "And charge extra," she says. "Because we're not a charity."

We go. The third note stays in its pocket like a promise that'll either pay out or collect. Either way, we'll be there when it counts.

The office smells of steam and solvent.
The pen is warm; the room isn't.
Blank space starts charging interest.

Chapter 28 — The Pen Decides

Morning behaves itself; the calendar doesn't.
Southend irons its shirt and forgets to mean it. We go back to the office by different pavements that agree to end at the same door.

The room pretends surprise, then remembers us properly. The heater tests our names and gets close on the second try. The box sits squared to the skirting, polite as guilt. The label stays blank—louder for being honest.

On the desk, the marker isn't where we left it. It's edged toward the blotter like a thought that prefers falling to planning.
Goldie taps the cap. "Still sealed," she says. "Still thinking."
Lola tilts it, checks the nib. "Dry at the lip," she says. "Someone tried a word and lost their nerve."
Trixie puts it dead centre. "Good. Let the room pick a side before the men do."

The kettle keeps its confession warm and unsaid.

At the corkboard: **PLATES?** still staring like a dare that ran out of breath. Under it, a fresh scrap leans wrong on one pin: **NAME**—and the question mark has crept in uninvited, the nervous hook tugging the word off-balance.
"Same hand," I say. "Same doubt."

Outside, a patrol car idles across the yard with teacher energy—lingers, judges, moves on proud of its restraint. It leaves patience behind like chalk dust.

Trixie slides the box a thumb's width. The tape lifts at one corner, not torn—tired. "Loyalty's losing interest," she says.
"Boxes learn our disappointments," I say. "This one's ready to

hand a few back."
Goldie doesn't smile; she edits her pockets. "Then we take the refund in full."

Lola's eyes do a slow circuit—hinges, sill, skirting, bin—then stop at the bin's lip. "Slip," she says, gentle as a cut.

We tip it out onto the blotter. Receipts, a dead elastic band, a corner of envelope with the same block capitals and that fidgety punctuation. **POST—** then a hook of a question that couldn't wait for its word. Below the tear: a single letter like a cough someone tried to swallow.

"Half a lie," Goldie says.
"Half a name," Trixie answers. "Worse."

The rails spend two notes through the window glass and keep the third for later. The room listens.

Lola nods at the door. "Audible shoes."
We hold our places. A man reconsiders courage on the other side and turns his route into silence. The handle tests a future, gives it back.

Trixie uncaps the marker, breathes once, then caps it again. "Honesty's a tool," she says. "Not a hobby."

We leave the label blank and let it shame the furniture. We leave the torn slip under a clean sheet where men keep their reasons. We leave the kettle on at the socket and off at the switch.

Outside, the river finishes somebody else's sentence and moves on without applause. The patrol car takes credit for peace it didn't make.

"Tonight," Trixie says. "Same room. We listen like furniture."
"Furniture with pockets," Goldie says.
Lola listens to the air choose a side. "And a pen that bites when it has to."

We walk. Southend pretends not to watch.
The third note stays pocketed—interest accruing.

Chapter 29 — River Watch

Evening irons the river flat, then leaves the creases where boats remember them.

We split like good news does—quietly. Goldie up toward the bridge. Trixie down by the slip, hands in pockets, listening to the air choose a side. Me on the railings, watching water pretend to be simple.

Truth forgets itself near water. I said it once as a joke. It kept not being funny.

The trick is remembering for it without leaving fingerprints.

Two gulls argue over nothing and win. Nets hang like old sentences. The tide thinks about fidelity and decides against it.

The rails push two notes across the forecourt and pocket the third. Private joke. Not tonight, then. Fine.

Down-river, Southend glows like a promise somebody else made. Up-river, London clears its throat and pretends it doesn't owe anyone. The wind edits people; it takes the parts they perform and leaves the parts they pay for.

Trixie doesn't look at me. She looks at the water the way you look at a mirror you can't afford—brief, honest, over. "We don't whistle," she says, not loud. "Not till we've earned the tune." Then she goes off with the kind of walk that makes policemen revise their notes.

I stay.

There's a van on the road above, not ours, not theirs, just van-shaped worry. It goes by pretending to have places to be. The river doesn't care. Rivers finish other people's sentences and move on without applause.

A woman leans on the far railing, framed by sodium. She sees her face in our faces and asks the window to lie. If she comes into our story, she'll come in sideways. Some people arrive like doors; some arrive like drafts.

Goldie signals from the bridge—two taps on the rail that read as weather. No patrol car. No Hartley proxy. Only us and the river and the third note waiting in its pocket.

I pretend to scratch a wrist and watch the dark where vans rehearse. Nothing rehearses. The dark keeps its secrets warm and unsaid.

The marker lives back at the office. The box does, too. Their loyalties are sleeping on the skirting, learning disappointment by osmosis. I like that about objects. They don't clap when you lie to them.

Boots behind me. One set. Honest weight. Trixie again.

"Window by the bait shed," she says. "Paper scrap. 'PLATES?' Same hand."
"Nervous hook?"
"Nervous hook," she says, and lets the river have her breath. "They're asking their questions on paper now. Safer than out loud."
"Safer for who?"
"For the room," she says. "Rooms hate to hear the answer."

We watch the shed. It doesn't do anything dramatic. That's the trouble with genuine tension—it behaves.

"Train'll spend the note when it matters," I say.
"Or keep it till the band's gone home," she says. "Same result if you're deaf."

A dinghy noses in against the slip. Two lads with haircuts that owe money; a third with a jacket that isn't his. They carry nothing carefully. Good. Not ours.

The woman down-river leaves by becoming colder air. She'll be back as someone else. They always are.

"Lay-by?" I ask.
"Later," Trixie says. "If they're bright, they change vans. If they're braver, they don't."
"Box?"
"Box stays polite," she says. "Until we're listening like furniture."

The river makes a small decision and comes a finger higher. Somewhere in Leigh a fridge hum turns into an argument and loses. The pier lights try flattery and succeed on teenagers only.

I press my palms flat to the rail. Metal is a teacher: it marks you absent and doesn't soften it.

"Lola," Trixie says without looking, "when this breaks, you're first through the silence."
"That a job or a compliment?"
"Same thing where I'm from."
She leaves the rest unsaid, which is the only way it has value.

Goldie descends from the bridge sideways, like a card you're not meant to see. She lights nothing; the lighter is a signal, not a flame. "Van with manners turned up twice, didn't stay," she says. "Teacher car wants to catch someone tomorrow, not today."

"So we give it homework," I say.
"Neat handwriting," she says. "Wrong answers."

A boat horn sounds like a throat clearing that cost money. The river smirks and eats it.

We settle into the shape of watchers. There are arts that never make a poster. This is one of them.

Watching isn't waiting; it's work the world mistakes for stillness.

"Tea?" Goldie asks.
"Office kettle keeps its confession warm," I say. "Might tell us something when the pen's ready."
"Pens don't talk," she says.
"They cut," Trixie answers. "Same result if you're careless."

The rails push the two notes again—closer this time, like the joke wants friends. The third stays buried. Not stingy. Patient.

A patrol car ghosts the road above and decides to be elsewhere. It hesitates the way teachers do when the bad kid's finally quiet—lingers, judges, moves on.

"Good," Trixie says, half-smile. "We stay quiet."

We take the long look. Shed, slip, vans, faces. Nothing moves wrong. The wrongness is punctual; it'll arrive when it said it would.

Goldie nudges my arm. "You hear that?"
"Wind in the bait fridge," I say. "Rope slapping a post."
"And?"
"And the room picking a side," I say. "Not ours yet. But not theirs."

Trixie breathes once, like a coin being counted. "We go back," she says. "We let the office remember it's ours. We make the label want ink."
"And if it doesn't?" Goldie asks.
"Then we teach it envy."

We turn as three and nobody sees us do it. That's practice. That's worth more than applause.

At the stairs I look back because somebody should. The woman is gone. The dinghy boys are jokes again. The river keeps its receipts.

Two notes. The third sits tight, a promise earning interest.

"Tomorrow," Trixie says. "Same room. Same pen. Less mercy."
"More tea," Goldie adds.
I don't add anything. I edit the night instead.

Southend pretends not to know us as we pass. We let it. Towns deserve their illusions. So do we.

By the time we reach the corner, the wind has finished with our coats and moved on to someone else's. A gull laughs like it's new to cruelty. The lights from Canvey practice hope on teenagers again.

At the office door, keys. Ordinary metal, ordinary turn. The kind of sound that gives men courage and rooms second thoughts.

Inside, the kettle's cold and smug about it. The box waits squared to the skirting, polite as guilt. The marker is where we left it—almost. Nearer the edge, like a thought rehearsing a fall.

"Tomorrow," Trixie says again, softer, to the room or the pen or the river pressed thin under glass. "We earn the tune."

The rails offer the two notes for free and save the third for the bill.

The night keeps the third note like a tab we'll settle in ink.

Chapter 30 — The Room Picks a Side

Night irons the street flat and leaves the creases where feet remember them.
We key the office like we own the lock. Ordinary metal, ordinary turn. The kind of sound that gives men courage and rooms second thoughts.

Inside, the air has saved our outlines. The heater tries our names again and gets them right on the second go.
The box waits squared to the skirting, polite as guilt. The label stays blank—honesty with a posture.

The kettle sulks on its stand. Truth forgets itself near water. The trick is remembering for it without leaving fingerprints.

Goldie flicks the light, then kills it, then lets the room pick a dim compromise. "Watching isn't waiting," she says, barely a breath. "It's work the world mistakes for stillness."
Trixie nods, eyes already on the desk. "Then we work."

The marker is closer to the blotter than we left it. Not far. Enough.
Lola tilts it, checks the nib with a surgeon's patience. "Wet," she says. "Someone thought out loud."

On the corkboard, the old dare still stares: **PLATES?** Underneath, a new slip at a wrong angle: **NAME?** Same block capitals. Same nervous hook on the question mark—as if the pen can't stop asking even when the man won't.

"Same hand," I say. "Same doubt. Different courage."

Trixie uncaps the marker, listens to the click, then caps it again. "The pen stays capped. The cut can wait."
Silence buys more than words do. Today we're paying cash.

We take positions you can only learn by losing:
— Goldie near the door, hip to the hinge, pocket lighter a signal not a flame.
— Lola by the desk, hands idle, attention spendthrift.
— Me at the window seam, where outside pretends it isn't listening.
— Trixie behind the blotter, a ledger in human skin.

The kettle breathes once—metal settling, or a confession clearing its throat.
"On," Trixie says. I nudge the switch. Orange eye. The room approves and pretends not to.

"I'll give it three sentences," Goldie murmurs.
"Two," Lola says. "The air wants a witness."

Footsteps outside. One pair. Then another that isn't sure if it wants to be a pair.
The handle tries a future, thinks better of it, and holds still like it costs money.

We don't move. We let the room decide whether we belong. The heater steadies. The compressor stops pretending and actually works. The kettle chooses a side and sends up a small ghost.

Belonging is a vote rooms cast in whispers.

"Now," Trixie says, soft as policy. She draws the box to daylight, peels the tape back a breath—not torn, just disenchanted.
Inside isn't evidence—it's a decision. A name that was never meant to be written, waiting to see who says it out loud.

We don't say it.

Lola slides a finger under the lid, not touching the contents, only the choice. "They rehearsed this box into being loyal," she whispers. "Tonight it hesitates."
"Boxes learn our disappointments," I say. "This one's ready to hand a few back."

From the yard: the patrol car ghosts by with teacher energy—lingers, judges, moves on. Chalk dust without a lesson.

The kettle finishes its sentence. Steam taps the cupboard door like a polite debt collector.
Trixie pours into four paper cups and doesn't ask who drinks.
"We mark nothing," she says. "We let the blank shame the furniture."
She places the marker dead centre. The room watches it the way crowds watch a tightrope.

Outside, the rails push two notes through the glass and keep the third for the bill.
"The night keeps the third note like a tab we'll settle in ink," I say before I can help it.
"Then bring a good pen," Goldie answers.

Lola turns her head a fraction. "Audible shoes. Deciding to be brave."
The handle tries again—half a thought, half a prayer. Stops.

Trixie breathes like a coin being counted. "If it opens," she says, "we laugh like rent's paid."
"And if it doesn't?" I ask.
"We still laugh," she says. "We just charge extra."

The laugh doesn't come. The courage leaves by the stairs.

We reseat the lid, leave the tape honest about its boredom, and put the box back where loyalty can see it.

Trixie sets the capped pen on the blotter's edge—a guillotine with manners.

We don't take anything. We leave the question marks to argue with their own hooks. We leave the kettle warm and the light almost off. We leave the room knowing it chose us back—tonight.

At the door, Goldie pockets the lighter without a spark.
"Furniture with pockets," she says.
Lola listens to the hallway breathe. "And a pen that bites when it has to."

Southend pretends not to know us as we go. We let it.
Two notes. The third accrues interest. Tomorrow we settle it in ink.

Chapter 32 — Lola, Foreground

Southend practises daylight like a piano piece—slow at first, then muscle memory. The river keeps its mouth shut, finishing other people's sentences where they can't hear it.

We take the long way to the office because Lola says the short way is full of men who haven't earned it. Goldie drifts the curb like smoke that bought shoes. Trixie wears her morning like a verdict she hasn't announced. I hold the street still by naming it—post boxes, chip shop, the window with taped cracks that look like a child's idea of lightning.

Lola owns the angle.

"Don't look at doors," she says. "Doors look back. Look at what doors make people do."

The office keeps our outline the way paper keeps a pressed flower—flat, lovely, a little dead. The heater remembers us second time. The compressor acts like a conscience that's been to therapy. The kettle waits with the patience kettles learn from grief.

On the desk, the marker sits capped where Trixie left it. The blotter has taken our weight and forgiven us for it. The box is squared to the skirting, label blank, tape scabbed, corners proud the way liars are.

Lola crosses to it and doesn't touch. She watches the air touching it instead. "They moved it," she says. "Half an inch back, quarter to the left. People who are sure never tidy their guilt."

Goldie leans at the hinge. "We opening it, or are we still pretending to be monks?"

Trixie studies the corkboard. **PLATES?**. Below it, that new slip with **NAME?** The question mark still hooks as if it wants to fish for an answer bigger than it can land. "Not monks," she says. "Bar staff. We pour what the room orders."

Lola tilts her head. "Then pour the kettle."

I flick the switch. Orange eye. Steam begins the hymn it knows. Truth forgets itself near water; Lola remembers it for a living.

She steps to the window seam and listens to the street breathe through its teeth. Then she speaks without looking at us. "We don't open the box," she says. "We let it open us a little. Enough to see what kind of people we are."

Goldie snorts softly. "Bad with refunds."

"Good with tabs," Trixie says, and nods at me. I slide the box a palm's width into the light. The tape gives like an old promise. The lid lifts a breath, the way a chest does when a name is almost spoken.

Inside isn't contents. It's a behaviour: a thinner sleeve, a card insert, a folded paper with lines where hands got careful. Names live there, or the idea of them. What matters is that someone decided the word "name" needed furniture.

Lola doesn't reach. She reads air currents like a pickpocket reading pockets. "They rehearsed here last night," she says. "Heard their own doubt and put it back with neat corners. That neatness will be their tell."

Goldie glances at the corkboard. "PLATES? NAME? You think same hand writes both?"

"The hand wants to be brave," Lola says. "The wrist won't allow it. The question mark twitches like it's ashamed of itself."

The kettle clicks through its last excuses. Trixie pours into four paper cups. No sugar. No milk. We drink like we're making a contract with heat. Lola doesn't sip. She watches the steam trace the cupboard door and memorises the way it lies.

"Lay-by tonight," she says. "Same van or a cousin. Different driver if they studied. The passenger will edit her face again. She's trying to be furniture. She's tired of being an ornament."

Trixie rests two fingers on the capped marker. "And us?"

"Crowd control," Lola says. "Of one room."

We don't talk for a minute. Not a silence—work. The kind the world mistakes for waiting.

Then Lola moves. A half-step to the corkboard, two to the desk. She uncaps the marker, listens to the click, then puts the cap back on. Ritual is a lock; sound is the key.

She writes nothing.

Instead, she drags her thumb along the outside of the cap and shows us the black crescent it leaves. "They didn't write yesterday," she says. "They thought about it and held on. People who say nothing leave ink anyway."

Goldie pockets her lighter. "People who say nothing get heard louder."

"Depends who's listening," Trixie says.

Outside, the rails push two notes across the morning and swallow the third. The day isn't stingy; it's saving up for someone who'll pay attention.

"Office later," Lola says. "Lay-by first. But before that—river."

We walk.

Southend keeps its head down the way guilty towns do when the sun is honest. The river is a lesson in finishing other people's sentences softly enough they think they finished them themselves. We stop where the railings have learned the names of elbows.

Lola rests her hands there and looks at the water like it owes her change. "Truth forgets itself near water," she says. "But it remembers faces. If she comes back to herself, it'll be here."

"The passenger?" I ask.

"She's practising not being seen," Lola says. "Sooner or later people practising visibility get tired. People practising invisibility get found."

Goldie fishes a rollmop out of a paper tub and grimaces like flavour is a dare. "Southend romance," she mutters. "He smelled like cheap cologne and rollmops—Essex in a jar."

Trixie takes one and bites it like she's punishing the word delicate. "Add whelks and cockles," she says, "and you've got the full tasting menu."

We eat properly, in silence. Salt, vinegar, a sweetness pretending it doesn't know what it is. The train gives us the two notes again and pockets the third like it's a ring it's not ready to sell.

Lola watches a reflection decide to belong to a woman or the river and choose the river. "Office," she says. "Then lay-by. Then whatever the box thinks we've earned."

Back at the desk, the room votes in whispers and chooses us again—for now. The calendar insists the date is the date; the little **PLATES?** slip insists doubt is tidy. The kettle is still warm enough to tell the same truth twice.

Trixie sets the box where loyalty can see it. "We're not opening it," she says. "We're letting it do its job. Boxes practice loyalty; we don't bully craftsmanship."

"And if the room turns?" Goldie asks.

"Rooms turn on you," Lola says, "but not for free. They ask you a question first."

"What's today's question?" I say.

She looks at the marker. "Who writes the name."

Nobody answers. That's also an answer.

We move out in the afternoon, the hour when towns pretend all their mistakes were morning ones. The lay-by wears yesterday's tyre prints like a necklace it didn't choose. Goldie takes her post at the crash barrier; Trixie pretends to study clouds; I catalogue the sound of the road until it gives me something it didn't mean to.

Lola counts the gaps between cars the way gamblers count their sins—one short, one long, then mercy.

The van chooses us the way the guilty choose a mirror—carefully, hoping the angle is kind. Different driver. Same caution. Passenger a silhouette that remembers being a face.

It rolls in. The gearbox introduces itself. Tail lights stay shy.

"Idle's lower," Lola says. "He thinks he's braver than last night. He isn't. He's exhausted."

The man in the hi-vis steps out, wearing a smile that doesn't belong to him; it hangs crooked, borrowed from someone who rehearsed better. He opens the passenger door a hand's width. The sleeve appears. Not heavy—careful. Names are a liquid; he hasn't learned that yet.

He hesitates. He wants an audience and is terrified of one. The passenger breathes like she's been charged per inhale. That isn't decoration. That's either in it or under it.

Lola lifts her chin a fraction. It's not a signal to us. It's to the moment. "Let him speak," she whispers.

He doesn't. He performs "thinking" instead—the big theatre of men who believe hesitation reads as wisdom.

Trixie's mouth becomes the idea of a smile. "Next time," she says, so quiet the grass has to lean in.

He slides the sleeve back inside, shuts the door, gets in, buckles his hope, pulls away. Tail lights keep not bothering; the gearbox does the monologue. He takes the left that is right. The rails push two notes across the sky and keep the third for someone with better timing.

We don't follow. Lola steps to where the tyres kissed the gravel and kneels. She doesn't touch. She lets the dust settle on its own and watches how it chooses to lie. Then she stands. "Office," she says. "The room will have rehearsed as well."

It has.

Inside, the chair at the desk sits slightly wrong—angled to the door, as if a man wanted to see trouble coming without letting trouble see he wanted to. The marker is centred precisely where Trixie left it. Too precisely. Men who tidy doubt overtidy props.

The kettle is cool. That's new. The heater ticks the way clocks do when they're ashamed of the hour.

Lola opens the box one breath. Inside, the inner sleeve is rotated. The folded paper sits one line higher. Not a signature—an alibi.

"Not heavy," she says. "Careful. But the care is tired. The box is learning disappointment."

Trixie rests a fingertip on the edge of the fold and doesn't lift it. "Who writes the name?" she asks the room softly, as if it could answer without losing face.

The rails try the joke early—two notes, then a silence big enough to rent out. The third will come when it wants to charge interest.

Goldie touches the corkboard with a knuckle. "PLATES?" "NAME?" "Whoever writes it first loses," she says.

"Or wins," Lola says. "Depends what game they think they're playing."

She caps the marker more gently than it deserves and sets it back, one millimetre off centre. A gift for a man who thinks tidiness is a personality.

We leave the box where loyalty can see us leaving it. We close the door in the tone of people who might be back or might not.

Outside, the river edits the light into something people can bear. The town practises ordinary. The train flashes by with two notes and a debt.

"Tomorrow," Lola says. "The box will choose a name. If it's ours, we don't say it."

"And if it's theirs?" I ask.

"We make them read it out loud," she says, and starts walking, quiet as a vow.

Two notes. The third accrues interest. We'll settle it when the pen moves.

Chapter 33 — The Name Decides

Southend puts its collar down and acts like wind was a rumour. The office doesn't—rooms remember what people try to forget. We let ourselves in the way you enter a church you don't pray in: hats off, backs straight, no speeches.

The kettle's cold but neat. Someone has been polite to it.

The marker sits a millimetre too centre. The corkboard wears its two soft questions like a matched set:
PLATES?
NAME?

Lola stands in the middle of the floor and listens to the air like it's a witness that hates court. "He came back," she says. "Same shoes as last night. Different courage. The kind that borrows from hope and pays back in interest."

Goldie does a hinge tour—one knuckle for each screw, a habit that looks like superstition and isn't. "Anything missing?"

"Only nerve," Trixie says, and rests a fingertip on the box as if it might run. Tape scabbed, corners proud. It has learned our pulse; it disapproves but keeps the secret.

I ease the lid a breath. Inside sits the inner sleeve, rotated nine degrees like someone measured doubt with a protractor. On top: a folded strip of paper. Not the old one. New. The fold has the tidy shame of a man who irons his mistakes.

Lola doesn't touch it. "Let it read itself first."

The rails push two notes through the morning, then swallow the third as if trains have private jokes and don't like company.

The heater tries to remember our names and mispronounces them; effort counts.

Trixie lifts the paper with two fingernails, the way you lift a moth you respect. There's ink. Not much—three letters and a mark that changed its mind. **CAL—** or **CAR—** The last stroke stutters into a nervous hook.

Goldie breathes out. "Question marks have a drinking problem."

"Same hand as PLATES," I say. "Same wrist telling it no."

Lola tilts her head. "He wanted to write the name and remembered he didn't own it."

Trixie lays the strip flat on the blotter. It sits there like truth caught between drafts. "The name decides," she says. "If it wants to be spoken, it will."

"Tonight?" Goldie asks.

"Tonight," Lola says. "But not in here."

The kettle gets the nod. I flick the switch. Orange eye. Hum. Water rehearses confession. Trixie pours into paper cups. No sugar. No milk. Heat as contract. We drink.

"Lay-by?" I say.

Lola: "Yes. But first—river."

We walk because walking edits thoughts cleaner than talk does. Southend practises ordinary through the station parade; nobody believes it and everybody plays along. On the railings by the river, elbows have embossed names; none of them match the one that won't be written.

Lola watches the tide finish sentences the town isn't brave enough to start. "If she's going to choose," she says, "she'll do it here."

"The passenger?" I ask.

"She's tired of editing herself," Lola says. "That either ends in a note or a name. We'll read whichever arrives first."

Goldie buys cockles out of habit and vinegar. "Essex sacrament," she says, passing the fork.

Trixie eats like someone punishing the word delicate. "If we sing tonight," she says quietly, "we start with 'Trouble.' Slow. No apology."

"Good," Lola says, not looking away from the water. "Let the room remember who owns the air before we borrow names from it."

The rails give us two notes and keep the third like it's saving up for a better story. We listen the way gamblers listen to luck when it pretends to be weather.

Back at the office, the light has shifted into the truth-telling angle—low enough to be honest, high enough to be kind. Trixie slides the strip back into the box and closes the lid the way you tuck a child in when you're not sure it's yours. The tape accepts the lie; loyalty is a habit before it's a virtue.

Goldie nudges the corkboard with a thumb. "PLATES? stays. NAME? gets company." She picks up the marker, uncaps it, thinks better, caps it again. "Not our handwriting."

"Not yet," Lola says. "Let him do his own courage."

Evening irons Monday flat and leaves the creases for us to read. The lay-by remembers us immediately; some places fall in love with the people who watch them.

Headlights comb the hedge. White panel van selects the gravel. Engine idles in the key of pretending confidence. Passenger present—the slice of a face that used to be a life. The driver wears a smile that doesn't fit and hopes the night won't notice.

We don't move. That's the job.

The window lowers two fingers. Air changes hands. The driver looks at a ditch that can't sign for anything. He reaches down, lifts something careful, places it on the sill: the inner sleeve. On top, folded once and bled through at the seam—a strip of paper.

Lola counts the heartbeats between his fingers leaving and his courage arriving. "Nine," she says. "He's early or terrified."

Trixie lets her mouth become the idea of a smile. "Both."

I step to the edge of seeing and no further. He edges the paper through the gap, pinched like a wasp that might be innocent. He doesn't look at us. He looks at the air and begs it to call him brave.

"Let him go," Lola whispers.

He does. Sleeve back inside. Window up. Gearbox tells the world what the tail lights won't. The van chooses left that is right and thinks it invented subtlety. The rails throw two notes into the dark and misplace the third on purpose.

We wait two full minutes because rituals are how you keep from lying to yourselves. Then Lola steps to the sill and takes the folded strip like she's accepting a dare.

Back in the office, the kettle pretends this is new. We don't humour it. Trixie lays the paper on the blotter and opens it.

The name looks like a person trying to pass for handwriting.
CALDER

No question mark. The last letter is a decision that cost someone a pint of blood.

Goldie doesn't swear, which is how you know it lands. "Well," she says softly. "That's one way to invite ghosts."

Lola touches the bottom of the **R** where the pen dug in and refused to be rescued. "He wrote it fast," she says. "Then slow, like a man walking past his own house twice."

I feel the old taste in the mouth—a metal that isn't cutlery. "Calder doesn't send his name," I say. "He arrives with it."

"He will," Lola says. "This is how he asks if we remember our manners."

Trixie closes her eyes and listens for a train that isn't due. "We do," she says. "We set the room. We sing 'Trouble' slow. We make the air ours before he thinks to rent it. Then we charge him for breathing."

Goldie taps the corkboard twice and adds a third against the wall—counting, not knocking. "And the box?"

"Loyalty on display," Trixie says. "Front of house. Stage left. Where names go when they want to be seen but not touched."

The heater finds its job for once. The calendar insists the date is the date; the little **PLATES?** slip looks embarrassed to be shallow. On the blotter, the name dries into itself.

Lola caps the marker and leaves it crooked, a gift for tidy men. "When he comes," she says, "he'll bring his own silence. We don't fill it. We price it."

The rails try the joke again—two notes, then the held breath that means payment due. Somewhere on a road that thinks it's smarter than maps, a gearbox clears its throat.

We stand the way people do when a room chooses them back and they have to answer without kneeling.

Trixie lifts the strip, folds it once, and slides it into the box as if boxes can be brave when people can't. "All right then," she says. "Let's give Calder a proper Essex welcome."

Goldie smiles without kindness. "Pepper. Vinegar. A bill."

Lola's eyes don't leave the door. "And the song," she says.

The office learns our shape again. Outside, Southend practises innocence for the night shift. The river keeps finishing what no one will say out loud.

Two notes. The third arrives when summoned.

We don't summon. We set the stage and wait like professionals.

Chapter 34 — Lola, Unfolded

The trick to waiting isn't patience—it's posture.

Lola leans on the railing by the estuary, coat collar up, one boot resting on the lowest rung like she's balancing time itself. The river's slow today, like it's carrying secrets wrapped in butcher's paper. Southend behind her is half-lit and half-interested, but Lola's not here for the town.

She's watching for echoes.

Calder's name has left the room, but not the air. The crew are playing quiet: Goldie's counting receipts that don't add up, Trixie's rewriting her mood in the mirror of the Half Pint's ladies' loo, and the Archive's closed its shutters like it never opened them in the first place.

But Lola… Lola listens to what the day edits out.

She's got a takeaway tea in one hand—lukewarm, lid missing—and the ghost of a laugh on her mouth that might've belonged to someone else. She doesn't sip. Doesn't need to. The cup's just a prop now. Something to hold instead of holding herself.

The river lifts a ripple and carries it east. She follows it with her eyes, like it's a line she's been waiting to read again.

"You always show up before it breaks," she murmurs, maybe to the water, maybe to the wind.

She reaches into her pocket—not for a lighter, not today—but for a piece of receipt paper folded like origami grief. She opens it. Three names. One's scratched out. One's circled. One's just a question mark.

She reads them like an old habit.

Trixie had asked her once, back when they were still pretending the job was about money: *What's the worst name you ever had to wear?* Lola didn't answer. But she carried the question with her, the way some people carry confessionals.

Today, she answers it silently, and folds the paper tighter.

From across the road, a bus sighs like it knows too much. The schedule's off again, but the people pretend it isn't. She watches them file on, some with their names clutched too tightly, some trying to leave theirs behind.

Lola watches.

She doesn't move until the third wave fails to break. Then she drops the receipt into the estuary and turns, finally sipping the tea. Cold. Bitter. Perfect.

By the time she steps into the alley behind the Half Pint, the box has already been moved. Trixie's scarf is gone from the chair. Goldie's lighter is warm, which means she's been checking exits.

Lola smiles. Just a fraction. Just enough to know she's still in it.

She's not the shadow.

She's the light that knows when to move.

The kettle starts to boil inside. And for once, it doesn't stop.

Chapter 35 — The Third Note

The Half Pint exhales us like a secret it's learned to keep. Chairs scrape, tills count, the landlord pretends microphones are saints now. We don't celebrate. We tidy—wires coiled like quiet snakes, the box lifted with two hands because history deserves manners.

"Two more," Goldie says, meaning the second set. "Then river."

"River first," Lola says, already listening to a distance. "Let it choose the order."

Southend pretends it's full. Monday never is. We walk the alley out back where deliveries become stories if you don't sign for them. The box rides in my arms, weightless in pounds, heavy in names. Loyalty's a habit; doubt is quicker.

Trixie leads without hurrying. Night gives her room like it owes her rent.

On the parade the wind tries on a personality and settles for blunt. The river has its lamps on—cheap promises from Canvey, a line of yellow lies pretending to be generous. People call it a view. People call lots of things by their politest names.

We take the rail like locals. Elbows find history. The tide mulls it over.

"Passenger?" Goldie asks, eyes on the station end.

"She'll come," Lola says. "People who edit themselves for a living always come to water. It forgives the crossings they didn't make."

"Calder?" I say.

"He arrives late," Trixie says. "So the night has to applaud."

The rails push two notes into the dark and keep the third like a bet they expect to win. The box sits on the balustrade a polite inch from falling and behaves better than most men.

A woman's silhouette peels off Southchurch Road and chooses the path like it belonged to her before houses did. The passenger. Hair pinned tight enough to keep a life in. Coat too good for the hour. She stops three paces back and breathes like the evening signed for it.

"Water doesn't care what I know," she says to the rail, not us.

"It cares what you write," Lola answers, still watching the tide. "Some letters sink louder than others."

The passenger steps in beside Trixie. They don't touch. The lamps make conspirators out of people who'd never say they were.

"I don't say names," she says.

"You carry them," Trixie says. "That's worse."

A car rolls by slow the way liars always do. It goes away because places like this have opinions and sometimes enforce them.

"What did he promise you?" Goldie asks, kindness turned down to a survivable wattage.

"Not to be recognised," the passenger says. "And then he said my name like he'd bought it."

"Calder's never owned a thing he didn't invoice twice," I say.

She looks at the box like it's a dog that could bite if loved wrong. "Is that…?"

"It's what people put things in when they don't want to hold them," Lola says. "Sometimes it tells the truth for them."

The river finishes someone else's sentence and moves on. The wind tries a new mood and is told no.

"I wrote a letter once," the passenger says. "It ended me. I never posted it."

"What did it begin?" Trixie asks.

"Debts," she says simply.

Goldie flicks the lighter without flame. Signal, not spark. "We don't take your debt," she says. "We price the air so he can't afford to breathe close."

The rails try the joke again—two notes, then the swallow. The third waits like a man in a doorway who thinks he's the plot.

Trixie looks at the water because it's the only thing honest enough to argue with. "You can leave," she tells the passenger, voice flat as law. "Tonight, tomorrow, when the letter gets bored of not being posted. You can leave under your own name, or under a quiet one we lend you for a week. But you don't stay and watch him spend you."

The passenger's mouth attempts courage. "If I leave, he writes me louder."

"Then we set the room to our volume and drown him," Trixie says. "Politely."

Lola nods towards the station. "He's decided the third note is his. He'll bring it when the night's ready to be paid."

The passenger turns to go, stops, returns one step, leaves a folded receipt on the rail. "I'm not brave," she says.

"You're punctual," Goldie says. "That's rarer."

The woman leaves the way clever people do—walking like she belongs to the street and not to the man who thinks he does. The river holds her reflection for three seconds, then lets it find its own legs.

Trixie takes the receipt but doesn't unfold it. "We don't rush what's already coming," she says.

"Second set," Lola says, as if the tide just told her the time.

Back in the Half Pint the air has learned us. People stand the way crowds stand when they've chosen to be an audience. The landlord has that look men get when money is happening and they'd like to pretend it's personality. The passenger is gone from her glass; the water remains, sweating for two.

I put the receipt under the box. Weight on weight. A promise under a habit.

"'Trouble' changed the lights," Goldie says softly. "They're not the same bulbs anymore."

"That's what law does," Trixie says, taking the stage. "It rebrands weather."

We don't call time. We begin because the night is finished asking.

Second set opens with something gentle that doesn't apologise. The kind of song that looks you in the eyes and counts your sins like tips. The room remembers how to listen.

Halfway through, the door learns a shape. He doesn't enter. He occupies. Calder wears the kind of stillness that thinks it invented patience. He looks at the box and pretends it's a coincidence. He looks at Trixie and pretends he's seen better. He looks at the room the way landlords look at land.

We keep playing. That's the trick. You don't greet weather; you hold the roof.

Lola slides a fraction toward stage left, as if giving the box room to declare itself. Goldie moves two steps toward the fire door and becomes architecture. I do nothing you can see.

Trixie finishes the song and lets silence arrive with its hat on. Then she smiles the smallest legal amount. "We'll keep this honest," she says, exactly as before, only sharper. "The night has its own requests."

She nods to the bass. The first note lands like a jurisdiction stamp. Not "Trouble" again. Not yet. Something older in her blood—sultry as a threat, precise as a bill. The room leans in because it has learned to.

Calder smiles with a mouth that doesn't belong to him. He doesn't clap. He prices. Men like him always think applause is a purchase order.

He steps inside only as far as the threshold allows. Good. Doors can do character work if you let them.

The rails push two notes under the roof. This time the third arrives—quiet, exact, final. The room hears it and doesn't know what it's heard.

Trixie does. She tilts her head like a falcon who's done the maths. "There it is," she says between lines, all smoke and arithmetic. "Evening, Mr. Weather."

Lola's mouth keeps its secrets but her eyes price the oxygen. Goldie doesn't blink enough to be rude.

We finish the number like professionals and let the quiet stand up and pay. Calder takes a step that thinks it's a favour.

The box doesn't flinch. It has decided loyalty is theatrical tonight.

Trixie's hand brushes the mic. "One more," she says. "Then we let the river speak for anyone struggling with consonants."

Calder stops smiling.

The room chooses us back. Outside, the water practises forgiveness. Inside, the third note hangs like a receipt that won't fold.

Chapter 36 — Let the River Speak

We don't announce an interval. We let silence choose it. Chairs shift like they're remembering manners; the till clears its throat and pretends money is personality. Calder stays where thresholds make men honest.

"Three minutes," Trixie says, not leaving the stage. "Enough to prove we don't run."

Goldie ghosts the fire door and listens for police that haven't been called. Lola steps to stage left and lifts the box a polite inch, then sets it down again—altar, not prop. The receipt I hid under it tries to escape like paper with a conscience. One corner shows a name that isn't signed.

"Keep it there," Lola says. "Truth behaves better with weight on it."

I slide alongside the bar as if I belong to plumbing. The landlord meets my eyes and decides this is a night for looking away at the right times. Out in the doorway, Calder practices stillness until it creaks.

Trixie leans to the mic but doesn't touch it, voice pitched for the front row and anyone with nerve behind them. "We'll start again when the room finishes the thing it's thinking." It sounds like mercy dressed as policy.

The passenger reappears at the edge of the mirror, hair pinned tighter than good sense. She doesn't look at Calder. She watches the water in her glass rehearse drowning and decides to let it.

Two notes slide under the roof as if the rails have learned to knock. The third waits outside with its hat in its hand. Payment pending.

"Now," Lola says, and the word agrees to be a doorway.

We move like regulars who know the short route. Back corridor, service yard, alley that edits footprints into shapes the council won't admit. Calder doesn't follow. He lets the night pretend it works for him. Good. Let him invoice the weather.

The river takes us without asking names. Canvey throws its catalogue of lies across the black and calls it hospitality. Wind tests the join in my coat and approves. We line the rail like a case file: Goldie watching the space behind us; Lola pricing air; Trixie giving the tide a chance to speak first.

"Third note?" I say.

"It's coming," Lola answers. "He thinks he carries it. He doesn't. The rails do."

Trixie places her hands on the cold metal and closes her eyes like it's a mic that remembers gratitude. "Say what you came to say," she tells the water.

A gull edits the sky. The river finishes somebody else's apology and lets it sink properly this time.

Footsteps. Not Calder. The passenger again, without courage's lipstick. She stands where a shadow could be blamed if needed. "He thinks you'll sing on command," she says.

"Then he's short a band," Goldie says, not unkind.

"I brought this." The passenger produces a Post-it folded four ways. It sticks to itself like fear. Inside: a number, a street, a time. In the corner: **PLATES?**—the same handwriting as the note by the Half Pint's till. The question mark hooks the paper like a nervous fish.

"He wrote that?" I ask.

"I did," she says. "He told me to remember the number. I wrote the question for me."

Trixie looks at the hook of the mark and nods once. "Good. Questions make better witnesses than people."

The rails push two notes as if they're small talk. The third rises from the station throat and refuses to be polite. It hangs over the river like a receipt that won't fold.

"There it is," Lola says, softer than weather. "Let it land."

Calder arrives on the parade without hurrying. He stops where men stop when they've learned that lines can be moved for them. He doesn't look at us. He looks at the space our looking makes.

"You've had your say," he calls, the kind of voice that thinks it invented statements. "Be finished."

Trixie doesn't turn. "We're not talking to you," she says to the water. "We're talking about you."

He takes two steps, the kind that cost other people. Goldie's lighter clicks once—signal, not spark. It tells him the distance is not decorative.

"Let him speak," Lola says, eyes on the tide. "He came all this way to fail."

Calder's smile arrives before his mouth. "If there's a box," he says, "it will be returned."

"It will," Trixie says. "To history."

He weighs the word like it owes him rent. "You don't know what you're holding."

"We do," I say. "A rehearsal. And a bill."

The third note drags a keel through the dark and pins the moment to the rail. The passenger flinches like a habit she thought she'd quit. Trixie reaches without looking and steadies the paper in my hand with one finger. "Read it," she says.

"Tomorrow," I answer. "Bad men count on urgency. We'll teach him Tuesday has ears."

Calder laughs like a door that's been asked to sing. "You want to play clever."

"We want to finish sentences you started," Trixie says. "This river's good at that."

He looks past us to see if the water will respect him. It doesn't. The lamps refuse to flatter his outline; the wind edits his coat until it admits to being just cloth.

"You'll regret it," he says.

"Regret's cheap," Goldie says. "We carry dearer."

Lola tips her head as if listening to a timetable only she has. "That's enough. He came to be seen. He's been seen."

Calder breathes the way people do when they're not used to earning air. He turns with the authority of men who think leaving is a weapon. His shoes count the boards too loudly. The river refuses applause.

We don't chase. Rooms turn on you; rivers don't. We let the third note fade into an argument it can win without us.

The passenger stays a moment past courage. "If I don't come back—"

"You will," Trixie says. "But if you don't, the letter won't mind."

The woman nods like someone who has finally put down something that wasn't hers to lift. She goes. The tide pockets her reflection and promises to keep it a week.

We hold the rail until the cold finishes its work. Then back through the alley where deliveries become stories. The Half Pint has gathered itself into an audience that thinks it invented patience. Inside, the box sits stage left, proud as old law. The receipt waits under it—the way truth does when it's decided to be helpful.

"Second set," Trixie says, stepping up. "We'll keep this honest."

Goldie takes the hinge tour; the door remembers its job. Lola adjusts the fan chain so the air will stay still when it chooses. I touch the fader like a priest who doesn't like churches.

The rails, generous now, send us the third note early. It arrives clean. The room hears it and behaves.

Trixie smiles a small, expensive smile. "Evening," she says into the ready quiet. "We'll start with a song that understands law."

She doesn't name it. She lets the bass say *Trouble* in a language the floor already speaks. The room leans. Calder is nowhere that counts. The river finishes our first line and returns the echo with exact change.

We are set. The night has its own requests. And the third note knows our names.

Chapter 37 — Billable Hours

We don't announce *Trouble.* We let the bass file it. The floor signs without reading. Trixie leans into the mic like it owes her interest and pays on time. Verse one takes the room by the jaw—no bruise, just the suggestion of one.

Calder is absent the way weather claims to be—felt, not seen. Good. Let the threshold do its job for once.

Goldie turns the fire door into a witness. Lola holds stage left like a compass set to *true north, no favours.* The box sits proud and quiet; under it, the receipt behaves like a promise that will need handwriting later.

Second chorus lands; the crowd chooses belief over curiosity. *That's all professionalism is—belief, rehearsed.* Trixie does the third line softer than law, harder than mercy. The room stops fidgeting. Tips recalculate themselves.

At the back, the landlord finally remembers he's Catholic about money and starts blessing the till.

We close the number without asking permission. Silence arrives with its hat in its hand; Trixie nods to it like an equal and steps half an inch back. "We'll keep this honest," she says. Same words, new jurisdiction. Applause chooses to be earned instead of spent.

Lola moves first, exactly three steps, and lowers the box from altar to arm—no rush, no mystery, just policy. Goldie ghosts past, checks hinge, bolt, latch, *people.* I fade the channel with the same care a priest gives a name he can't pronounce and won't stop trying.

"Five," Trixie says under breath—meaning minutes, meaning miles, meaning *not now, not him*. She turns to the room and gives them a song shaped like a lullaby that learned to carry a knife. You don't fight a storm by shouting; you make the roof listen.

The passenger's glass sits where she left it—half water, half reflection. The mirror returns no statements.

Between numbers, the doors admit two new men who are paid to look like they belong to nobody. Their shoes tell the truth—*civvy-police, off the clock, on a favour*. They don't look at us. That's how you know we're in the picture.

Lola sees them and edits nothing. "Tuesday has ears," she says, words for us alone.

Goldie counts the bodies like a card sharp who already knows the trick. "Back room after this," she murmurs. "No lights, kettle off."

Trixie runs the room by tone, not volume. She picks something with a spine and no swagger—lets people think they chose to be quiet. That's the art: make obedience feel like taste.

I watch the threshold where Calder isn't. *Absence with edges.* Men like him love an entrance more than a victory; when they don't get one, they invoice the nearest sky.

Song done, we don't bow. We fold. Chairs sigh. The landlord names the next drink after relief.

Back room. The kettle stands accused. The calendar insists on the present. On the corkboard, the same shaky **PLATES?** hook tries to look casual and fails. I put the box down on the table where wood remembers elbows and decisions. The receipt goes beside it, unfolded to the number, the street, the time. Nobody reads it out loud. Names travel worse when spoken.

Lola lays both palms on the lid—not to open, to steady. "He wants us rushing," she says. "We'll be punctual instead."

Goldie checks the window like it once lied to her and got forgiven. "Passenger's clean," she says. "Left the way clever people do."

Trixie sits without relaxing. "Two officers in the house," she says. "Their boss owes someone a favour."

"Which direction?" I ask.

"Us, for now," she says. "Debt wants to be admired before it gets collected."

The box sulks with good manners. It doesn't flinch. Boxes rarely do until you teach them disappointment.

Lola lifts the lid a quarter inch—just enough to let the air remember paper. Then down again. "Still a rehearsal," she says. "Still a bill."

"Tomorrow," I say, tapping the receipt once—*ink has its own pulse*. "Eleven. We don't arrive early to other people's bad ideas."

Goldie pockets the Post-it copy she made while our eyes were elsewhere. She doesn't brag. Professional theft is just memory with good penmanship.

We give the kettle no power. We stack cups in the sink like a set of small refusals. Trixie fixes her lipstick with the kind of accuracy surgeons hope for and stands. "Last set," she says. "Then sleep that means it."

Out front, the men who look like nobody have chosen a table that thinks it's furniture. Their hands behave themselves. Good boys. The crowd's drank itself into listening; *best kind.* The passenger is gone, but the shape of her seat knows what it saw.

We climb back onto the little stage that never forgives shoes. The room chooses to keep us. Trixie takes the mic like a handshake she means. "We'll keep this honest," she says again, because some rituals need to be notarised thrice.

Goldie's lighter clicks once—signal, not spark. Lola nods to the rails no one can hear from here. The third note answers anyway, late and exact.

We play the kind of number that sends hearts home safely and minds nowhere good. Trixie tells the truth in a key nobody can sue. People clap like they're paying a bill they don't resent.

Between songs, the door learns the outline of a man who almost walked back in and didn't. *Good boy, Calder. Learn restraint while it's on offer.*

The night finishes correctly. We sell records we don't have and accept thanks meant for other sins. The landlord counts, re-counts, and tries to look like a patron instead of a till with shoes.

Closing. Chairs on tables. A wet cloth confesses across the bar top. The two off-duty drift to the threshold and pretend their timing is weather. One of them touches two fingers to his temple in a gesture that could be respect or arithmetic. We accept both.

Alley. Southend practices empty. The wind is done with auditions. Out by the rail, the river has gone tight-lipped; even

Canvey's lies take a night off. We don't linger. We're not romantic about exits.

At the car, Lola rests the box on the back seat and straps it in. "Names travel safer when they think they're passengers," she says.

Goldie slides into the front with the map in her head. "Tomorrow, eleven," she says. "Borrowed time, borrowed names."

Trixie looks at the dark like it's a stage waiting for a soundcheck. "We'll return what isn't ours," she says. "And charge for the labour."

I drive. The rails try two notes for us as we cross them. The third saves itself like good whiskey.

Halfway home, the kind of car that wants to be followed appears in the mirror and decides not to be brave. It turns off where cowards turn off—into a street that sells courage retail and regret wholesale.

"Calder?" Goldie asks.

"His paperwork," I say. "Not his face."

Lola watches the window like it's a transcript. "He'll try courtesy next," she says. "Men switch tactics when the room refuses applause."

"Let him," Trixie says. "Courtesy leaves fingerprints too."

We pull up outside a building that thinks it's survived worse. Inside, the stairwell smells of old mail and older arguments. Our door knows our knock. The flat lets us in because loyalty is easier for bricks.

On the table, we clear a square big enough for truth to sit without sulking. The box goes there. The receipt goes under one corner like a shim for a wobbly future.

Trixie takes off her jacket and doesn't hang it. "Sleep," she says, not as suggestion. "Tomorrow we stop pretending Tuesday is polite."

Goldie checks the chain, the bolt, the night. Lola draws the curtains in a single smooth sentence. I turn the kettle *off* to make sure it's heard.

Lights down. City hum. Somewhere, the rails send a third note to somebody else's roof. Good. Spread the gospel.

In the dark, Trixie says it like a closing line that hasn't picked its chapter yet: "We'll keep this honest."

Nobody argues. Tomorrow can.

Chapter 38 – Ink Doesn't Lie

The pen arrives with no fanfare. Just a weight in the room and a pause that edits the air. It's black, no logo, cap off—like it never needed permission.

Trixie doesn't touch it. Not yet.
Goldie's hands stay flat on the table. Lola leans back, reading the ceiling like a confessional.

"No clipboard?" Trixie says, dry.
"No clipboard," I say. "No forms. Just the bit that matters."

The box is open, but not empty. Names weigh more once they've been written, and this one's been rehearsed—flattened, folded, nearly forgotten.

Lola watches it like a witness, not a judge.

Trixie finally picks up the pen. Not like she's signing. Like she's holding a fuse.

"Anything you don't want in ink," she says, "say now."
Goldie doesn't blink. Lola doesn't breathe.

The train outside gives us one note, waits, then offers the second. The third is missing again. Not gone—**held**.

"Don't write it," Lola says suddenly.
Everyone turns.

She's not stopping us. She's just saying it like a weather warning.

Trixie's hand hovers.
"Why?" I ask.

"Because once it's down, it's not just a name anymore," she says. "It's a witness. It remembers. Ink doesn't lie."

The pen hangs in her grip.
Then she writes.

Slow. Careful. Letters that shape the next three moves, the next ten regrets.

The name lands. Full. Undeniable.
The paper doesn't flinch, but we do.

Trixie caps the pen, sets it down like evidence.
"Done," she says.
"No," Goldie says. "Started."

Chapter 39 – The Procession

The day doesn't start. It permits itself.

Southend's light is thin but precise, like a scalpel left on a windowsill. The river has stopped rehearsing. The air wears gloves.

Trixie stands outside the Half Pint, coat collar up, shoes unpolished on purpose. Goldie lights nothing and looks like she meant to. Lola watches the street the way a safecracker watches seconds—measured, criminal, reverent.

She blinks slow. One breath. Two. Then murmurs, "It's begun."
Not a warning. A timestamp.

"On time," Goldie says, though no one's moved.

"They want us ready," Trixie replies. "They want to think we need the money."

The van appears first—same tailgate, same apology. This time it brings manners. And quiet.

No engine rev. No horn. Just arrival.

A city that knows how to behave.

The back opens like confession. Two men climb out, wearing suits that don't quite fit their necks. One carries the box. The other carries belief. They scan the street the way debt collectors scan faces.

"They don't trust the room," Lola says, calm as logic, eyes narrowed.

"They shouldn't," Goldie replies.

The crew lets the men walk the pavement alone. They do it badly—feet too loud, eyes too fast. Southend narrows for them, closes shutters, straightens bins. The barbershop's blinds twitch once and then pretend they didn't.

Lola doesn't blink.

"They'll lie before they speak," she says. "Watch for the apology in their hands."

At the door, the men pause—like they expect it to speak first.

"They're stalling," Trixie says. "Trying to see the price in our posture."

"Let them," Lola murmurs. "We're not selling posture. We're charging for patience."

Inside, the Half Pint has already rearranged itself. The stools stand in witness. The air keeps a tally. The ink's dry but still talking.

The men step in like they've earned it.

They haven't.

One sets the box on the table. The other nods as if that counts.

"Delivery as promised," he says.

Goldie doesn't answer. She just opens the top flap.

The box doesn't move.

Not hesitance. Not fear.

Just… memory.

Trixie places one hand near it—*not on it*—like you would with a wounded dog. "This box knows things," she says.

"It's a container," the man says.

"No," Lola answers, softer than breath. "It's a witness. And it's listening."

She's holding the marker now. Uncapped. Upright. Reverent. It rests in her hand like it knows it won't be used lightly.

The second man clears his throat—once, twice, then swallows it. "Where's Calder?"

"We don't summon weather," Goldie says. "We price it."

And then Calder walks in.

He's not late. He's not early. He arrives with the weight of someone who's already seen how this ends and doesn't like it. His coat is too clean. His eyes are busy.

He looks at the box.

He looks at the marker.

He looks at Lola.

She doesn't flinch. Doesn't blink.

She tilts her head half an inch, studies his shape like she's looking for the lie beneath the tailoring.

He tries *courtesy* first—small nod, slight smile.

She edits her face with surgical precision—removes the welcome, keeps the recognition.

The room doesn't offer him a chair.

"We have terms," he says finally, as if it's a favour.

"You had terms," Trixie corrects. "Then you borrowed names."

Lola steps forward. She doesn't write. Not yet.

She just lifts the marker—and the word is on her breath, not the page. Not yet.

Calder's smile cracks, just at the edge.

"You don't know what's in there," he says.

"We know what's not," Goldie replies. "And that's enough."

Silence. Then a train passes, two notes only.

The third is absent. Not swallowed.

Withheld.

Like the river's watching.

Like the air's waiting.

Like Lola already knows what the word will cost—and has priced it anyway.

Chapter 40 — The Word

No one moves first. Not Calder. Not the men beside him. Not even the box.
Only the marker.

Lola lowers it gently to the table. Upright. Uncapped. Waiting.

Trixie steps aside—not giving ground, just offering air.
Goldie watches Calder like a locked drawer.
Me? I count the seconds that aren't being spent.

Lola's fingers rest near the box. She's not afraid of it.
She's listening to it. Like it's a story halfway through confessing.

"It's just a word," Calder says.

"No," Lola replies. "It's *yours*."

The river outside says nothing. But it leans in.

The bar hums with withheld judgement. The beer taps gleam like a warning.

Goldie leans forward, chin in her hand. "We're not here for ink," she says. "We're here for *truth spelled properly*."

Calder doesn't blink. "You're bluffing."

"No," says Trixie. "We're *publishing*."

Lola lifts the marker.

It hovers for a second—the weight of what it's about to do pressing down like gravity with an opinion.

And then: the stroke.

Not loud. Not rushed.

She doesn't write a name. She *unearths* it.
Letter by letter. A word that knows how to wait.

The box doesn't flinch.
But Calder does.

He moves as if something just let go inside him.

Trixie doesn't look at the word. She looks at Calder. That's where the reading is.

"You didn't plan for that," Goldie says. "You rehearsed everything except the one thing that stuck."

"It's not finished," Calder says.

"It is," Lola says. "You just haven't caught up yet."

The men with him don't speak. They're looking at the word now like it's not meant to be seen in daylight.

One of them mouths it, and it doesn't sound like English anymore.
It sounds like *owed.*

The bar breathes out.

The box settles—not lighter, not heavier. Just *known.*

"You could've asked," Calder says, low.

"You could've told," Lola replies, softer still.

There's a silence, and this time it's earned.

Trixie slides the marker back into its cap.
Goldie folds the paper.
I close the box—not to hide it, but to finish the sentence.

"We'll let you decide how the story ends," Lola says.

Calder doesn't speak. Doesn't blink.

He leaves with the word still on the table.

The bar doesn't follow him out.

It just keeps the echo.

Chapter 41 — The Invoice

The pub holds its breath the way old buildings do when memory walks in. No sound, no gesture—just the weight of something arriving that shouldn't.

Trixie's got one hand on the ledger and the other on time. Goldie's mouth tightens like it's read the last page already. Lola? She's still. Still like stone. Still like scripture. Still like someone who doesn't ask the room for permission.

Calder doesn't sit. He browses the air like it's a menu he wrote himself. His coat's damp at the hem—must've been waiting outside, deciding what sort of man to be.

"I expected fire," he says.

"You're not flammable," Trixie replies. "Just borrowed."

He looks at the paper Lola left on the table. The word still sits there, black and calm and impossible. It doesn't accuse. It doesn't explain. It just *is*.

He reaches for it, but Goldie clears her throat. Not loud. Just enough.
"Price first," she says.

"You want money?"

"We want honesty," Trixie says. "Money's just how liars measure shame."

He smiles. It doesn't reach his eyes. Or maybe his eyes are too busy watching exits.

"I thought you were professionals."

"We are," Lola says. "That's why we invoice before we explain."

She slides a second sheet across. It's blank. But Calder flinches like it's full.

"What am I paying for?"

"For the time we didn't waste," Goldie says. "For the names we didn't write. For the rooms we didn't break."

"For the truth," Lola says. "The bit you buried in someone else's accent."

The pub lets in a breeze—enough to move the curtains, not enough to be trusted. Somewhere outside, the river coughs up its third note. Finally. It's early, or it's late, but it *knows* now.

Calder finally speaks to the word on the table.

"That's not my name."

"No," Trixie says. "It's your *invoice*."

He looks at the blank sheet again. This time, he doesn't reach for it.

"I'll need time."

"No, love," Goldie says, and lights a match without lighting anything. "That's what ran out."

He leaves with his coat open, like it's too late to close anything. The paper stays. The name stays. The room exhales and clocks back in.

Nobody says much.

Lola picks up the blank invoice, folds it once, twice, three times, and slides it into her pocket. Maybe it'll be needed. Maybe it won't. But some receipts don't need numbers.

They just need to *exist.*

Chapter 42 — The River's Change

The river doesn't hurry. Never has. It trades in patience, in stories that skip stones and never break surface. By the time we reach it, the tide's out but watching — like it's waiting to be convinced.

Lola stands a few paces ahead. She's not in a hurry either. Her boots find the edge of the embankment where the railings turn lazy, and her fingers hover above the bar like she's waiting for it to whisper first.

Behind us, the station shrinks. Ahead, the estuary flattens the sky. The crew doesn't speak yet. Even Trixie holds her coat closed like it's not the wind she's guarding against. This isn't a mission. It's a reckoning.

"I used to think the river finished other people's sentences," Trixie says. "Now I reckon it starts them."

Lola nods once. Just once. Then reaches into the satchel—the one that never slouches—and pulls out the box.

It's smaller than you remember, every time. Smaller, but heavier with names.

Goldie leans on the railing. "One of them's gonna try and take it back," she says. "You know that?"

Lola doesn't blink. "Let them try. It's already remembered too much."

The box rests between them now. Not opened. Not yet. The wind does a loop, tucks itself behind Lola's ear and whispers nothing useful.

We don't form a circle, not quite. More like a bracket. Holding space. Holding silence.

She opens it like it's fragile. Like the truth might bruise if you lift it wrong.

Inside: paper, folded. Ink still bold. Lola lifts it with both hands.

She reads it once, doesn't read it again. Doesn't need to.

"It's time," she says.

And then she turns to the river — that slow confessor, that quiet witness.

"Do you want it to float?" I ask.

"No," she says. "I want it to be remembered. So we let it go where it'll be misfiled."

She tears the paper — not angry, not rushed — just enough to break the shape without breaking the weight. One half goes in first. The river hesitates. Then takes it. The second piece follows.

"You think that's enough?" Goldie asks.

"No," Lola says. "But it's a start."

Trixie lets her breath out through her nose. "If Calder wants it back, he can dredge it himself."

"No he can't," Lola says. "Not anymore."

We stay a while, until the river forgets our names again. And when we leave, it's not because we've finished.
It's because the river has.

Chapter 43 — Weight in the Water

The morning doesn't rise; it shoulders its way in like it's returning something it borrowed.

The Thames is mute today. Not silent—just choosing not to speak. The tide's out, the bank's exposed, and the river wears yesterday's silt like a confession it hasn't quite signed.

Trixie stands on the slipway in boots that don't flinch. Goldie sits on the low wall behind her, hands in her lap, lighter unopened. Lola stands to one side, jacket off, sleeves rolled, one foot bare in the shallows. She's not washing—she's measuring.

"Any last words?" Goldie asks. It could be a joke. Could be a liturgy.

Trixie doesn't answer. She watches the current the way a gambler watches a last card—not for what it is, but what it means.

Lola lifts the box. Not reverently. Not like it's sacred. Like it's overdue.

The weight of names is uneven. That's why they rattle.

"It'll float," Goldie mutters. "Only if it thinks it deserves to," Lola replies.

They step into the water together. Not far. Just enough. The mud complains, but allows it. Trixie kneels. Lola opens the box.

The river doesn't flinch. It watches.

Inside the box: paper, files, a name circled too many times, a verdict scribbled sideways, a receipt, a story, a strategy. The marker sits on top, capped. Not ashamed. Just done.

Trixie takes one page. The name. She folds it once, twice, and presses it flat with her thumb. Then places it on the water.

It doesn't float. It accepts.

"Don't follow it," Lola says. Not to Trixie, but the river.

Goldie lights the lighter this time. Doesn't smoke. Just watches it burn down.

Behind them, Southend hasn't noticed the weather shift. Buses run. A dog barks at its own echo. Somewhere, a kettle forgets to boil.

Trixie stands. The box goes under.

The river doesn't take it. It holds it.

That's the difference.

Some truths get buried. Some get archived. And some get watched until they stop trying to be remembered.

They step back. Goldie pockets the lighter. Lola rinses her foot. Trixie checks her collarbone like it's a compass.

None of them look back.

But the river does.

And for the first time in three chapters, it gives them the third note.

High. Clean. Unasked-for.

Like a name finally returned.

Like a story that agrees to end.

Chapter 44 — Small Hours

The river doesn't rush tonight—it waits.

Outside the Half Pint, bins huddle like they know something, lids angled against the wind like guilty shoulders. The sky's trying to remember how to be black instead of grey. Somewhere east, something's coming—but not yet.

Inside, silence isn't awkward. It's earned.

Trixie's mug is cold. Has been for a while. She hasn't said a word since she came down the stairs with her shirt inside out and her necklace backwards.

Lola notices. Doesn't mention it. Just edits the moment with a glance and lets it pass, like a priest skipping a verse out of kindness.

Goldie's already at the window, lighter in hand but not flicking it. Just holding it. Thumb resting like she's pressing a bruise for memory.

None of them talk about last night—not what was done, or what it meant, or who started the sentence and forgot to end it. It's not denial. It's protocol.

"I'll check the car," Lola says, too casually, and steps into the chill.

Goldie finally looks up. "She all right?"

"She slept," Trixie says.

That's all. But it's everything.

Goldie nods. One of those nods you give to a choice that's already been made, and a consequence you're willing to take tea with.

Outside, the wind tests the bins again. One lid clatters—like it heard something it shouldn't have.

Trixie lifts the cold mug, doesn't drink. "You think they'll call?"

"They already have," Goldie says. "They're just waiting to see if we blink."

A train hums in the distance. Two notes. No third.

Lola comes back in. Doesn't take her coat off. Doesn't sit down. "Tyres were touched," she says. "Just a brush. Just enough."

"Message?" Goldie asks.

"No," Lola says. "Memory."

Trixie finally smiles. "They remember us?"

"No," Lola says. "They remember who they weren't."

The room adjusts its temperature. Accepts the silence again.

This isn't aftermath. It's betweenmath—the breath before the next ask.

Outside, the river stirs like it's heard a name it wasn't supposed to know.

And inside, three women stand still long enough for the room to choose them again.

Chapter 45 — The Shape of the Ask

The air tastes like it's been folded, like the day was pressed in a book and forgotten for years. Southend doesn't blink. It watches.

Trixie's coat is creased from sleep that wasn't hers. She's pulled together, but only just. Shirt buttoned right this time, but the necklace still reversed. Maybe on purpose now.

Goldie hasn't said much. That's her apology.

They sit at the cafe with the small menu and the bigger silences. The waitress brings tea unasked, like she knows what they've been running from.

Lola watches the door, not the window today. "They'll send a question," she says. "They'll want it to feel like a choice."

"But it won't be," Goldie replies. "They never ask what they can just test."

A kid outside drags a stick along the railings. The rhythm's off—stutters near the end. That kind of day.

Trixie flips her spoon over three times before speaking. "We say no. This time. Whatever it is."

"And if it's not a question?" Lola asks.

"Then we still say no," she says. "Just louder."

Their food arrives. Beans already apologising. Toast sliced on a slant that suggests the knife was tired.

A van idles across the street. No plates. The kind of idle that listens.

Goldie doesn't flinch. "That's not ours."

"No," Lola agrees. "Ours hasn't blinked yet."

They eat like it's strategy. Bite, scan, bite. The street begins to twitch with people who pretend they aren't pretending.

Inside the sugar pot is a folded note. Same handwriting as the one from the Half Pint: block capitals with no sense of humour.

One word.

"TONIGHT."

Trixie folds it twice. Once for now. Once for later.

"Where?" Goldie asks.

"Where we started," Trixie says. "Before the box. Before Calder. Before the names started thinking for themselves."

Lola nods like it's geography, not fate. "Back to the origin, then."

"And what do we bring?" Goldie asks.

"Just the invoice," Trixie says. "And the answer."

They don't rush. There's time. That's the worst part. Too much time to plan, not enough to rehearse.

The waitress brings the bill, folded like a prophecy.

They leave it on the table.

Let the debt collect interest.

Chapter 46 — Folded, Brewed, and Barely Buttoned

The morning wasn't in a rush. It buttered the streets slowly, let the bins clatter without apology. Overhead, a gull laughed like someone who'd slept too well and knew it.

Trixie sat on the back step with a tea that hadn't steeped long enough to argue. The shirt she wore was Goldie's. It tried to pretend it belonged there, but the buttons knew better.

Inside, Goldie hummed something half-remembered and twice as dangerous. The tune smelled of trouble and tasted of someone else's lipstick. She moved like she'd earned sleep and spent it all on secrets.

"We don't talk about it?" Trixie asked without turning.

Goldie didn't answer, but the kettle did—a whistle shy of confident, like it had caught them mid-thought.

"Right," Trixie said. "We fold it up, same as laundry. Just warm enough to pretend it never wrinkled."

Goldie leaned in the doorway, hair still wet, expression folded into something unnameable. "You said that like it was poetry."

"I said it like it was Essex."

They didn't touch, but the space between them steamed like it wanted to.

The rest of the crew was due at the Half Pint by nine. The clock knew, the walls knew, even the floorboard under Goldie's left foot knew. But they didn't move.

Outside, a van reversed badly into yesterday's promise. Inside, Trixie drank her tea like she hadn't made a decision yet. Goldie lit a cigarette without lighting it. Ritual, not habit.

"We'll have to tell Lola," Trixie said.

"She already knows," Goldie said, tapping ash that hadn't formed.

Silence followed, respectful as a locked drawer. Then Trixie stood, slow and deliberate, like she was choosing not to flinch.

"We don't have to name it," she said.

"No," Goldie replied, folding the word like a receipt. "But we'll know if it goes missing."

By the time they left, the morning had folded itself into shape. The bins were done arguing. The sky held its breath. And the shirt—still Goldie's—pretended it had always been worn inside out.

Chapter 48 — The Fold Knows First

Some mornings start like a shrug. This one starts like a held breath nobody dares to claim. The cafe doesn't open for another hour, but the door's unlocked because the kettle said so.

Trixie leans against the counter, shirt inside out again, though no one's naming it. Her collar's turned like a question no one asked, and Goldie's hair carries the kind of shine only laughter or sin can explain. Lola wipes the table twice, not because it's dirty—but because repetition feels like control.

No one mentions the shift. That's how real things stay real.

"We're early," Goldie says, not looking at the clock.

"The day was waiting for us," Lola replies. "Didn't want to be the one to knock."

A newspaper lies abandoned on the next table, headline folded inward like it regrets something. The crossword's half done. Three across: *Place where silence speaks loudest (5).* Nobody tries to solve it.

Trixie pours three cups and says nothing. The kettle hums like it knows the end of the story and doesn't want to spoil it.

Outside, the street yawns into life—bins rattle with purpose, and a man with a clipboard scolds a van for being parked like a confession.

The silence isn't awkward. It's seasoned. It's the kind that grows roots.

Lola reads the steam like tarot. "The box moved," she says.

Trixie nods once. "Without us?"

Goldie shrugs, but her mouth is set. "With permission we didn't give."

The air buckles for a second, the way it does before a song starts—or a fight.

"You ever wonder," Trixie says finally, "if the box was always gonna move? Whether we walked it there or not?"

"The box listens," Lola says. "But it doesn't wait."

The door squeals open. Not for drama—for honesty. A girl in a green mac steps in, clutching something wrapped in brown paper. She doesn't speak, just looks at them like they've already said yes.

Trixie gestures to the table. Goldie gets up without a word. Lola places a napkin down like it's an oath.

The girl sits. Unwraps the paper. Inside: not a name, but a photograph. Black and white. Bent edges. Four faces. One of them is Calder. The others are not.

Trixie takes it, barely glances. "You kept the receipt?"

The girl smiles like she doesn't want to. "You're the only place I could return it."

Lola tilts her head, studying the curve of the paper. "The fold knows first," she says. "That's where things break."

The girl nods, stands, leaves without her tea.

They don't follow.

Trixie slides the photo under her saucer. "We've got a day, then."

"A full one?" Goldie asks.

"No such thing," Lola says, wiping the table again. This time, it's clean.

Chapter 49 – The Hum

Part One: The Fold

The room doesn't start—
it waits.

Curtains that were drawn stay that way, like they've made a pact with the dark. The air smells faintly of burned toast and hesitation. No one owns the silence yet, so it lingers, like a dog not sure which human is meant to call it.

Trixie folds yesterday's paper. Doesn't read it. Just folds it again.

Goldie runs her thumb over the edge of a cup, watching for a chip that isn't there. "You sleep?"

"No."

"Same."

Lola doesn't say anything. She's watching the ceiling like it's hiding messages in its cracks. Her jacket's on the back of the chair. Inside out.

The kettle hums.
Not boiling. Not done.
Just a hum. Like it's listening.

Trixie stands, re-buttons her shirt—wrong buttons in the wrong holes. Doesn't fix it. Sits again. "It's nearly today."

Lola finally moves, brushes hair from her face, lifts the cup, sets it down. Doesn't drink.

Goldie stretches, spine clicking like an old lock. "Any news?"

"No," Trixie says. "But the room's quieter than it should be."

Outside, the bin lorry reverses with a whine that feels like a complaint, not a warning. A man shouts at a dog. A door slams two streets away and sounds personal.

The kettle hums again. It's not in a hurry.

Lola reaches for the folded paper and doesn't unfold it. She just smooths it flat, like she's pressing down on something trying to get out.

"I think today's the day it doesn't come," she says.

"What doesn't?"

"The third note."

They sit with that. Not arguing. Just measuring it.

Trixie finally gets up and pours three cups. None of them drink.

The hum stops.
Not a click. Not a whistle.
Just… stops.

The quiet feels final.

"Alright then," says Goldie, rising slow. "Let's go disappoint someone."

Part Two: The Shift

The morning walks beside them, not ahead. The pavement smells of Sunday arguments and cheap polish. Bin bags slump like they've given up waiting.

The crew moves without choreography now—
not lost, just unscripted.

At the junction, they stop. Same as always. Same as never. The train mutters two notes behind the buildings, but it's not trying this time.

"There's no third note," Lola says again. "Not today."

Trixie nods. She adjusts the collar of her coat, like she's dressing for something less official than fate.

Goldie lights nothing. Just flicks the lighter once and lets it cool in her palm.

They don't head for the usual place.
They don't say where they're going.

But the air gives way, like it's heard this plan before.

By the time they reach the back lane—the one with the graffiti that lies flatter than memory—they know what the knock will sound like before it comes.

It does.

Three taps.
Two breaths.
No speech.

Lola opens the door this time.

Not to invite.
To witness.

The room inside is smaller than it should be. Boxes sulk against the far wall. One of them is open—but not revealing. Not yet.

The kettle there is cold.

Trixie walks to it anyway. Lifts the lid. Doesn't fill it.

"Let it hum when it's ready," she says.

Behind her, Goldie checks the box—not the contents, but the shadow inside it. "Still waiting."

"Good," says Lola. "So are we."

They don't sit.

They don't close the door.

They wait with the box.
Not because it's time.
Because they'll know when it is.

And outside, in the wind that's forgotten how to hurry—
the third note does not come.

Chapter 50 — The Long Receipt

The office smells like tomorrow's argument: damp ink, cooling metal, something left too long unspoken. The heater clicks once, twice—then gives up pretending. Silence creeps back in like it paid for the room.

Trixie's coat hangs off the chair back, half-arm in, as if she's only borrowing the moment. Goldie nurses a tea that's forgotten its temperature. Lola stands by the window with one hand tucked into her sleeve, the way people do when they're trying to stop remembering.

On the desk: a single sheet of lined paper. Top left, a date that hasn't arrived yet. Top right, a name that isn't theirs. Beneath it, itemised silence.

Lola breaks it. "Calder's man watched the platform all night."

Trixie doesn't look up. "Good. That's time he can't charge anyone else for."

Goldie turns the cup slowly, like she's trying to stir time. "He's not trying to find us. He's trying to find the invoice."

"The word?" Lola asks.

Trixie finally looks up. "No. The cost."

A train wails in the distance. Two notes. No third. It's been missing all week. The air feels like it's waiting for someone to admit something.

"We can't hold this forever," Lola says. She's not asking. She's measuring.

Trixie shrugs without moving. "We don't have to. Just long enough."

Goldie raises a brow. "And what's long enough?"

"When the weight stops shifting," Trixie says. "When Calder starts folding his silences instead of offering them."

Outside, the street stretches like a yawn that's seen too much. Inside, the list on the desk waits: six names, four dates, three places that no longer answer their own phones. A seventh name is pencilled at the bottom. The paper doesn't shake, but it wants to.

Goldie leans closer. "You sure about the last one?"

"No," Trixie says. "That's why it goes last."

The door creaks, but no one enters. It's just the wind trying to remind them of its presence.

Lola places her hand flat beside the paper. "This is the long receipt," she says. "Not what we owe—what we carried."

Trixie watches her, then nods. "Fold it once. Then let it hum."

They leave it on the desk, folded. Not sealed. Just enough to say: we remember.

And then they walk out—not in formation, not in flight—but the way people do when something sacred has been said and nobody wants to be the echo.

Chapter 51 — The Folded Note

The note was folded once, not twice. That mattered. A second fold would've meant privacy. This one meant promise—unfinished, unhidden.

Goldie sees it first when she circles back for her lighter. It's not where they left it. It's moved—only an inch, but enough to say it had company. The desk's surface holds no dust, just the faint outline of a palmprint that didn't mean to speak.

She doesn't touch it. Not yet.

Downstairs, the kettle hums like it remembers who asked the question last. Lola stands next to it, eyes closed, hand resting on the windowsill. The steam rises slow, steady, like a name being coaxed from a throat.

"You heard it too?" Goldie says when she comes in.

"I felt it," Lola says. "Paper shifts when it knows something."

Trixie is outside. In the alley. In the rain that isn't sure whether to stay or leave. She's lighting a cigarette and not smoking it. Watching a bin bag that's caught on the wind, turning in place. The lighter doesn't click—she just holds it, flame paused, like punctuation.

Inside, the kettle goes quiet. Goldie takes the folded note, flips it like it might bleed if opened.

Still only one fold.

"Read it?" Lola asks.

"Not yet," Goldie says. "Reading is final. This is still rehearsal."

A train shrieks in the distance. One note. Then silence.

"Not even two today," Lola says. "It's folding itself shut."

The note sits between them, casual and treasonous. It doesn't hum, doesn't twitch. But the room does. A twitch in the floorboards. A breath from the cupboard.

Trixie steps back in and peels her wet coat off with a sigh. "If the room's listening, let it hear this."

She walks to the note, lifts it, doesn't open it—just looks at the fold. She smiles, just slightly. "It's enough."

Lola doesn't ask why.

Goldie doesn't press.

The room folds around them.

And the third note? It doesn't come. Not yet. But the silence it leaves behind… hums.

Chapter 52 — One Fold, Two Shadows

The note isn't opened, but it travels.

Trixie tucks it into her coat like it's always been there, a receipt from a life she's still pretending was hers. No ceremony. Just friction against the lining, and a sigh the note doesn't mind.

They walk.

Lola takes the middle—not centre, just middle. She walks like the pavement owes her rhythm but not explanation. Goldie drifts left, where the railings play wind chimes with last night's bottles. Trixie leads, or follows, depending who's asking.

Southend folds in on itself. Shopfronts blink tired neon. A dog barks at nothing and gets nothing back. The van with no plates doesn't reappear, but its shadow does—across a puddle that chooses not to reflect.

"They'll think the note says everything," Goldie mutters.

"It doesn't," Trixie says.

"What does it say?"

"Just enough."

That's the weather today: enough.

They pass the café with the one-legged sign. It sways, but doesn't fall. Lola stops. Points to the window with her chin.

Inside: Calder. Not pretending to be someone else today. Just sitting. Reading a menu like it owes him a favour. The waitress ignores him with professional grace.

He doesn't see them.

Trixie doesn't look away.

Goldie lets her hands drop into her pockets like holsters. "Do we?"

"No," Trixie says. "Not yet."

Lola tilts her head. "He's waiting for the third note."

"He'll wait all day."

They move on.

By the river, silence waits in puddles. The sky tries rain but gives up after two half-hearted drops. The wind carries smells that don't match the season.

Trixie leans against the wall and finally speaks to the air.

"If it ever opens," she says, "it'll bleed."

Goldie offers a half-smile. "Paper or us?"

"Depends who flinches first."

Lola takes the note from her coat without asking. Runs a finger along the single fold. Doesn't open it. Doesn't read it.

But for a second?

She looks like someone who already knows.

Chapter 53 — The Folded War

Calder watches like a man who's learned to wait for earthquakes—not to stop them, just to know when to hold his glass.

He doesn't speak when he arrives. Doesn't ask for a table. Just finds a booth near enough to hear the radiator complain about the cold. Places his coat beside him like a fourth guest and lets the silence arrange itself.

Trixie clocks him once, brief as a blink. Doesn't nod, doesn't stiffen. But her fingers go to the edge of her coat. The fold's still there—untouched, unread—but Calder has always known that the most dangerous things don't need to be opened to be weaponised.

He marks it.

Not the note itself—he never sees it. But he sees the *space* it holds. The way Lola stands when it's near. The way Goldie avoids her own reflection. The way they all make room for something that has no name on the register.

He finishes his tea. Doesn't touch the saucer. Slides a receipt from his pocket—nothing written, just creased once down the middle.

He folds it again. Slower this time. Then sets it on the table, dead centre, and leaves it there like a bet.

Nobody comes to collect.

Later, the waitress picks it up. No tip, just the fold. She doesn't open it—maybe because she's polite. Maybe because she isn't.

The fold is still whole. But now it's **plural**.

Chapter 54 — The Receipt of Things Unsaid

The table hasn't moved, but it feels further from the door.

Trixie fingers the fold through her coat pocket like it's a coin too warm to spend. Lola watches the sugar packet someone tore in half and left behind—white grains spilled like unspoken names. She doesn't brush them away.

Goldie drums her fingers once, twice, then stops. Her lighter stays pocketed. No sparks today. Just weight.

"He clocked it," Lola says.

Three words. No tone, no accusation—just weather.

"He didn't touch it," Trixie says.

"Didn't have to," Goldie murmurs. "He folded one of his own."

They don't ask how she knows. They never ask that sort of thing anymore.

Outside, the wind clocks off and leaves the sky unsupervised. Southend does its impression of harmless. Bin lids rattle like gossip too tired to lie.

The fold inside Trixie's coat weighs nothing but holds everything. Not just the word, but the *right* to it. She hasn't opened it. Might never. That's not the point.

"He writes now," Goldie says.

Lola nods. "Badly."

The tea arrives. No one ordered it, but the waitress knows. She places the pot down like she's placing a bet, then leaves without asking questions. The pot steams like it's trying to forget.

Trixie pours. The tea lands clean. "We don't fold again," she says. "Not until we're ready to open."

Goldie stirs without sugar. "And if he folds first?"

"Then we let him," Lola says. "Some people fold to disappear. Some fold to detonate."

A silence settles. Not awkward. Measured. The kind you wear to a funeral you're not sure is yours.

Later, when they leave, the table is spotless—except for the one folded napkin Lola leaves behind.

It doesn't say anything.

But it knows who it's for.

Chapter 55 — The Note That Wrote Itself

They don't talk about the napkin.

Not on the walk. Not in the van. Not in the lift with its hiccuping hum and graffiti that's been politely ignored by four councils and a priest.

But the silence has chapters now. Bound and numbered. Cross-referenced. Calder's note isn't a threat; it's worse—it's polite.

Goldie flicks through CCTV on a cracked monitor. "He left it under the plate. Folded twice, corner-tuck. Show-off."

Lola watches the feed like it owes her a memory. "Corner-tuck's theatrical. Wants an audience."

Trixie doesn't speak. She holds a biro like it's a blade and stares at the pad they've all been too clever to use. One blank sheet. No header. No logo. Nothing but nerve.

"He's not guessing," she says. "He's mirroring."

"Like a bad magician," Goldie says, "with worse timing."

The room smells of yesterday's takeaway and today's hesitation. The note—*his* note—sits unopened in the centre of the table, daring them to fold back.

Lola crosses her arms. "He wants it opened. That's the play."

Trixie shakes her head. "No. He wants it *guarded.* He wants us to carry it like ours. Make it *mean.*"

They don't touch it. Not yet.

Later, when the building sleeps and the city reverts to factory settings, Lola takes it with tongs and drops it in a steel tin. Not destroyed. Not preserved. Just *paused.*

She labels the tin in pencil:
"Received, Not Accepted."

And under that, in smaller script:
"We fold for truth. Not theatre."

The next morning, they find a receipt under the wiper blade. No amount. No logo. Just a scribble where the total should be.

One word.
Written in *her* handwriting.

And she didn't write it.

Chapter 56 — The Receipt That Wasn't Yours

The table's too clean. That's how you know it's wrong. Pub's half-empty, but the air sits packed—folded in on itself like it's waiting to be unfolded by the wrong hands.

Goldie taps a beer mat like it owes her change. Trixie watches the clock, not for time, but for confession. Lola's eyes don't track—they *hover*, like they're choosing what not to see.

There's a receipt on the table. It doesn't belong to us.

Folded, yes. But wrong.

Too neat. Too new. Edges like it *meant* something.

"I didn't order that," Goldie says, voice half-joke, half-check.

"You didn't," Trixie replies.

No one touches it. That's important.

Outside, the bus lingers at the lights like it knows who's aboard and isn't sure it wants to stop. Inside, the landlord wipes a clean glass clean again. Twice.

"He's copying," Lola murmurs.

"Copying what?" Goldie says, but doesn't want the answer.

"Our quiet. Our fold. Our signal," Lola says. "But he doesn't know how to carry it. He's using the moves, but not the music."

"That receipt's got the wrong ink," Trixie says. "And he's written in it already."

No one checks, because checking is how you get trapped.

The jukebox coughs up a slow tune that's forgotten its chorus. Calder's not here—but his scent is. Paper, boot leather, and that aftershave people buy to smell expensive to themselves.

"I think he left it," Goldie says.

"Or he had someone leave it," Lola adds. "He's building a choir of echoes."

Trixie shifts in her seat like she's rearranging armour. "One fold too many and the paper cuts back."

The receipt stays. So do we.

A couple by the window argue in sign language. It's fluid, sharp—more honest than most conversations that use mouths. One of them gestures "stop," but the other replies with something that looks like *"too late."*

The lights flicker once, not from power, but from *choice.*

Lola leans in, quieter than a tactic. "He thinks he's inside our ritual. But he doesn't know who the priest is."

Goldie cracks her knuckles like punctuation. "We burn it?"

"No," Trixie says. "We reply."

She pulls a napkin. Folds it. Writes nothing. Leaves it beside the receipt. The bartender watches too long and then forgets to look.

Outside, the third note *doesn't* arrive.

That's how we know it's working.

Chapter 57 — The Fold War

Rain behaves itself—for now. It makes a polite noise against the pub's windows like someone knocking on a door they hope won't open. Inside, the receipt and the napkin sit side by side: one eager, one empty.

We leave them both.

Trixie leads, coat shrugged on like a sentence she hasn't finished. Goldie's a half-step behind, fingers curled and ready. Lola doesn't walk so much as ghost—shadows pause to let her pass.

The fold war has rules. But Calder's rewriting them.

"He's rushing the ritual," Lola says. "Faking the silence without earning it."

"Faking the ink," Goldie mutters.

Trixie doesn't speak. Her mouth is a vault.

At the station, a man tries to sell us umbrellas. Says the sky's a lie and the plastic's the truth. We walk past him like we're water.

On Platform 2, the third note *does* arrive—but it's early. Clumsy. The rhythm's off.

"That's Calder," Lola says. "Playing with timing like he knows the tune."

"He doesn't," Trixie replies. "He just wants to be louder."

The train door opens with a hiss that sounds like disapproval. We don't get on. The passengers do—faces half-folded in on themselves, lost in screen light and wet coat smells.

Goldie watches a man fumble his season ticket. "You reckon he's watching now?"

Trixie nods once.

There's a poster on the far wall: *Missing Cat. Answers to Echo.*

"That cat," Lola says, "has more sense than Calder."

A receipt flutters by—not *ours*. But folded. Wrong again. No writing. No grease. Just suggestion.

Trixie picks it up. Turns it once. Folds it tighter.

"Time to reply," she says.

They follow.

We don't go back to the Half Pint. We go to the *other* one—where Calder won't know the light, or the exits, or how the silence sits in the rafters.

Lola lays out the booth like it's court. Goldie arranges condiments like they might vote. Trixie orders tea—no milk, no sugar, just steam.

Then she unfolds the napkin.

Still blank.

She writes one word.

Not a name.

Not yet.

She folds it once, then twice. Passes it to Lola.

"Your move."

Lola adds nothing. But she creases it differently. Goldie nods like she's seen a verdict pass.

We leave it under the cup.

As we exit, the waitress picks it up. Reads nothing.

Calder will think he's received something. That's his first mistake.

He'll reply.

That'll be his second.

The third? Well.

That note's still folded.

Chapter 58 — The Third Mistake

The rain comes back like it remembered something rude. Not wild—just thorough. The kind that doesn't want attention, just obedience.

The booth's empty now, save for steam, crumbs, and the folded napkin we left behind.

But Calder's already touched it.

We know because the fold's wrong. His fingers crease with impatience, not ritual. The paper sits wrong—like it's uncomfortable being understood too quickly.

Lola clocks it first. "He's copying handwriting now."

Goldie raises an eyebrow. "His or ours?"

"Neither," Trixie says. "He's trying to invent one."

We walk the long way, past the shop that sells keys nobody ordered and the dry cleaner that stopped pretending the stains were removable. Every door holds its breath as we pass.

By the river, the tide's out but the weight remains. Not the water—what the water remembers.

Trixie stops at the railings. "He's guessing," she says. "About us. About the note."

Lola nods. "Guessing makes noise."

Goldie lights a match and lets it burn down to thought. "We fold. He unfolds. That's the difference."

A receipt flutters by, soaked and shapeless. Not ours. Not his either. The city's own attempt at silence.

We find the next delivery spot on instinct. A takeaway that used to be a chapel, still smells faintly of confession and vinegar. The chairs are plastic; the truth isn't.

The man behind the counter nods at Trixie. He doesn't ask. He just hands over a white paper bag folded with care. Loyalty, pressed flat and steaming.

"Paid in advance," he says.

Trixie smiles like a sealed envelope.

We take it to the bridge.

"Now?" Goldie asks.

Trixie shakes her head. "Almost."

The napkin is with us. The one Calder mishandled. It carries a lie now—his.

Lola leans over the railing. "Let the river decide."

Trixie nods.

The napkin drops.

It doesn't float. It lands like a thought no one wants to own. The river swallows it without interest.

"That was his third mistake," Lola says. "He thought folding was the same as knowing."

Behind us, someone coughs—too polite to be a stranger.

We don't turn.

Trixie just speaks into the rain. "Tell him the river keeps receipts. Just not his."

Goldie cracks her knuckles like punctuation. "We're up."

Lola pulls her coat tighter, then looser again. Like she's learning the shape of the next silence.

The third note plays on the wind—almost right this time.

He's learning.

That's what worries us.

Chapter 59 — The Girl with the Inside-Out Shirt

There's a time of day—just before the bins clatter and just after the birds give up—that belongs to no one. Southend holds its breath like it knows something's coming, but won't say when.

The Half Pint opens early, not because it needs to, but because silence likes a head start.

Trixie's first in. She's wearing yesterday's shirt—inside out. The label shows at her shoulder, a small, white confession that says everything and nothing. Goldie isn't far behind, collar damp, hair twisted like she wrestled the night and let it win on points. They don't speak. That would make it real.

Lola's already in the back. She's folded into a chair like she invented posture and got bored halfway through. She looks at Trixie once, then doesn't look again. That's how you protect a secret you didn't ask for.

"Calder's been," Goldie says eventually, dropping the words like a pin she hopes won't roll. "Left nothing. Took nothing. Just… air."

Lola stands. "That's worse."

"He saw the fold," Trixie says. Her voice is hoarse in a way that isn't tired. "Didn't open it. Didn't touch it. Just… acknowledged it."

Goldie flinches. Not big, but enough. "He's getting clever."

"No," Lola says. "He's getting ritualistic. That's different. That's worse."

They move through the morning like it's a tightrope over a truth they've already denied. Tea gets made. Seats get taken. The room decides who it belongs to, and today it's split.

On the bar, the kettle hums without boiling. It knows better than to raise its voice.

"We deliver today," Trixie says. "That's not up for debate."

"Even if he's watching?" Goldie asks.

"Especially if he is," Lola answers, and it's not defiance—it's choreography.

There's a new note in the room. Not music—just pressure. The kind you feel in your teeth.

Trixie brushes her fingers over the hem of her inside-out shirt. She doesn't fix it. That would be an apology.

Outside, the bins begin their clatter. The day has started. They stand.

They've got something to deliver, and someone to answer.

And the label on Trixie's shirt flutters like it's proud to be caught.

Chapter 60 – The Quiet You Can't Return:

The delivery is not dramatic. That's the point.

It's the way Lola holds the box like a memory too old for questions. The way Trixie counts steps, not seconds. The way Goldie watches reflections instead of people. It's the choreography of certainty—deliberate, unspectacular, absolute.

The drop site is a narrow corridor behind a shuttered arcade. The kind of place that keeps its secrets under bubble wrap and last year's signage. It smells like old copper and wet cardboard—somewhere between danger and detour.

The box goes down like it knows its job. Palms flat. Corners square. Respect, not reverence.

Nobody speaks.

Nobody has to.

The silence is not awkward—it's contractual.

A man watches from across the road. Calder. Of course it's Calder. He doesn't approach. He nods once, like someone pricing a suit in a shop he can't afford. Then he walks away.

"Let him," Lola says. She's not asking permission.

Trixie doesn't watch him go. She adjusts the box a fraction, so it sits in shadow.

Goldie places a receipt beside it. Not for them—for the silence. That's what they've traded.

Back at the Half Pint, the kettle boils without warning. It doesn't whistle. It hisses. The steam curls like a question they won't answer.

Trixie removes it from the heat. No tea. Just silence.

They sit in it.

Calder doesn't come back. Not yet.

But the box stays exactly where they left it.

And that quiet?

That quiet is the kind you can't return.

Chapter 61 – Ink Will Remember

Some names don't echo—they stain. The kind you rinse, scrub, file, forget—only for the paper to hum back hours later, dry and unforgiving.

We sit in the Half Pint, but not really *in* it. The place feels borrowed. Calder's last receipt curled in Trixie's pocket like a dare, and the folded note—ours—waits without blinking, its silence sharper now. It knows we've read it, even if we haven't opened it.

Lola pours the tea, deliberate. No sugar, no milk. The hum is gone today. Or maybe it's listening.

Goldie doesn't speak. Not out of protest—more like conservation. Every word now costs.

Trixie thumbs the edge of a coaster until it bleeds damp. "He's not waiting anymore."

"No," Lola says, gentle. "He's preparing."

The city outside holds its breath between shift changes and bin runs. The type of pause that always means someone's buying time, or selling it.

Trixie stands. Smooth, practiced. The kind of movement that carries a name in its pocket and dares the world to guess it.

"I'm going to the river."

No one asks why. The river has a job now. It finishes the sentences nobody dares speak aloud.

By the river,

It's near-empty, mid-tide. That part of the day when even the mud looks like it's reconsidering its loyalties. She stands alone this time. No lookout. No crew. Just Trixie and the truth, whatever shape it's taken today.

The box isn't here. But the weight is. Still wrapped, still waiting.

She closes her eyes. Her hand finds her jacket pocket. A note folded once. Then again.

She doesn't open it.

Instead, she breathes.

Long. Sharp. Decisive.

Behind her, footsteps crunch gravel. Not careful. Familiar.

Goldie.

She doesn't speak. Doesn't have to. The presence is enough to tilt the air.

Trixie offers the note without turning.

Goldie steps beside her, not in front. That matters.

Together, they watch the tide flirt with the bank. A whisper of boots. A second of breath caught between years.

Then—

Goldie places her hand on Trixie's back. Warm. Steady. That kind of touch.

Trixie leans back—just an inch.

Enough.

Later, when they walk away from the river, the note is still folded. Still unread.

But its shape has changed in her pocket.

And so has she.

Chapter 62 – The Hand That Doesn't Shake

Some hands tremble when they lie. Others when they write. Trixie's does neither.

We're back in the Half Pint, but this time it's holding us properly—like it's stopped judging, and started preparing. Chairs creak like they know secrets. The kettle hums a little early. The note stays folded on the table, but its presence is louder now, like a witness who's changed their mind about staying quiet.

Lola enters last.

She doesn't speak. She *sets*. The chairs, the light, the angles. It's not ritual—it's curation. A gallery of silence and consequence.

Goldie leans with one elbow on the table, fingers drumming a code none of us can crack. "We charge for lateness now?"

"No," Lola says, smoothing her jacket. "We invoice it."

Trixie doesn't smile. But her mouth remembers how.

"Did he clock the note?" Lola asks.

Goldie nods. "Didn't read it. Just *clocked* it. Like he thought it might read *him* first."

"That's when he got dangerous," Trixie says.

"He was always dangerous."

"No. Before, he was *sharp*. Now he's *curious*."

Curiosity's worse. Sharp you can anticipate. Curiosity lingers, watches, asks questions in quiet corners and makes strangers remember your name without ever meeting you.

Trixie pulls the folded note closer. Not to open. To feel.

"He'll send another," she says.

Lola nods. "And we'll return to sender."

Outside,

The street wears Thursday like a confession. Too early for payday. Too late for excuses.

Trixie stands outside the pub like she owns the sky above it. She lights nothing. Says nothing. But the air behaves differently around her.

Goldie steps beside her.

"You alright?"

"No," Trixie says. "But I remember how to act like I am."

They watch a boy post a letter. Watch him walk away lighter. Like paper carries weight *only* when you keep it.

Lola joins them.

"He's moving," she says. "Saw him clocking the betting shop. Not for money—for *names.*"

Trixie sighs. "Then he's ready."

Goldie pulls out a pen. The good one. The one that doesn't forgive spelling mistakes.

"Let's write something he *won't* rehearse for."

They don't laugh. But the wind does, brushing past like it's read the next few pages and likes where it's going.

Chapter 63 – Strike Price

The sky forgets its colour and borrows from bruise. Southend smells of damp receipts and late decisions.

Trixie stands in the centre of the Half Pint's back room, not posing—posting. A declaration without a stamp. She's marked the edges of the table with chalk, not for ceremony, but for jurisdiction. The kettle isn't plugged in. That's on purpose.

Lola's at the window. Not watching—*measuring.* Her eyes track people by rhythm, not direction. You can lie with your body. You can't lie with your gait.

Goldie's just come back in from her smoke. The kind you don't light for pleasure—just punctuation.

"Today's not for doing," she says. "It's for costing."

Trixie nods. "He'll offer terms."

"And we'll invoice his assumptions," Lola says, softly.

There's a pause—room-sized. The kind that holds breath like it's drawing interest.

A knock. Not eager. Not polite. A knock with a mortgage behind it.

Goldie doesn't move. "Third note?"

"No train today," Lola says. "The station held its tongue."

Trixie crosses to the door. She opens it with one hand and silences it with the other.

Calder stands in the threshold like a man who's learned where the trap is and steps into it anyway.

He's holding a note. Folded. Sharp.

Trixie doesn't reach for it.

He places it on the table.

It lands with the weight of a cheque and the smell of old ink. There's a red pen mark through the fold—not to cancel. To call attention.

"You've named your price?" he asks.

Trixie doesn't answer. She looks at Goldie. Goldie looks at Lola. Lola edits her expression.

"Yes," Trixie says finally, and the room exhales like it's been holding that syllable for weeks.

Calder tilts his head. "Shall I read it?"

"No," Goldie says. "It's not for you."

"Then what am I doing here?" he asks.

"Watching value accrue," Lola murmurs.

The kettle hums, even though it's not on. Just memory. Or menace.

"You don't get to decide when this ends," he says.

"No," Trixie replies, calmly. "We only decide who charges interest."

He leaves without another word, but the note stays. Folded. Untouched.

The crew doesn't move for a full minute. Then Goldie picks it up, turns it over, and slides it under the box like a signature under a statement.

The chalk marks on the table blur just slightly. Not erased—*earned.*

Chapter 64 – The Room with No Corners

Southend again, but not the part that makes postcards. A narrow backstreet pretending it forgot its own name. Rain has done the maths and decided we owe it something.

We wait in a room that doesn't have corners, not really—just slow conclusions. The walls are the colour of breath held too long. Ceiling yellowed by choices nobody's owned up to. A plug socket with no plug, like a metaphor nobody dares finish.

Trixie sits on the edge of a chair like it might bite. Her hands are still, but her shadow shifts. Goldie leans against the window and lets the glass chill her spine, a kind of confession. Lola stands. Doesn't perch, doesn't flinch. She reads the room like scripture—quiet, complicated, unedited.

"This where they'll come?" Goldie asks.

"No," Trixie says. "This is where they'll think we were."

A kettle hums in the corner, not plugged in. Some rooms remember.

There's a knock, but not at the door. A knock somewhere deeper—plumbing maybe, or nerves.

"They know we've seen it," Lola says.

"The word?" Goldie asks.

Lola doesn't answer. She opens her hand to reveal a folded napkin. Not the one from before—a new one, creased with intent. Written on it: **one line**.

"Is that yours?" Trixie asks.

"No," Lola says. "It's theirs. They're mimicking."

Goldie swears without using her mouth. The kind of swear that hangs in air and unbuttons fate.

"This changes things," Trixie says, but doesn't sound surprised.

"No," Lola says, quiet. "It reveals them."

We don't touch the napkin. We let it sit, centre stage, like a trap we're still naming. The kettle ticks like it's agreeing. Outside, the rain lifts slightly—just enough to hear footsteps choose not to come any closer.

Lola tilts her head. "They don't want us to respond."

"They want us to react," Trixie corrects.

The difference is everything.

We leave the napkin on the windowsill. Let the night find it. Let the city decide if it's litter or evidence.

As we step into the dark, the walls don't follow.
That's how you know the room has chosen sides.

Chapter 65 – Duplicate Keys

The Half Pint holds its breath longer these days.

We enter in shifts, not fear, just practice. The kind you pick up when someone learns your rituals well enough to parody them. Goldie checks the hinges. Lola listens to the silence. Trixie stares at the bar like it owes her a name and hasn't paid up.

The back room smells wrong.

Not broken, not ransacked—*wrong.* Like someone opened a box, read the air, and folded it back badly. The heater's still ticking. The paper's still stacked. But the kettle's cold and full, and that's how you know someone's been uninvited.

Trixie closes the door with the kind of quiet that comes after a scream. "How did they get in?"

"No forced lock," Goldie mutters, running her fingers under the rim of the desk. "No new scratches."

"Duplicate key," Lola says. Not a question. "They watched us long enough to forge access. Or bought it from someone who sold memory for cash."

Trixie lifts the lid on the archive box. It *hesitates.*

The papers are still there. But one has been turned. Not removed, just *considered.* The way you do with something you think you've earned but haven't paid for yet.

"They're mimicking *our* restraint," Lola says. "Same fold. Same patience. Different purpose."

"They're mocking us," Goldie says.

"No," Trixie corrects. "They're *rehearsing*. There's a difference. Mocking is noisy. This is… measured."

She lifts the paper, reads the crease. Whoever touched it wore gloves, but not out of caution—out of reverence.

"They *believe* they're part of it now."

Lola steps to the kettle, turns the handle, lets it hiss. "They're not."

"Not yet," Goldie adds. "But they're writing their own script."

A flicker in the mirror behind the bar—someone's reflection? Or just the building remembering a face from last night? Trixie doesn't blink.

"We change the locks," she says.

"We don't use locks," Lola says. "We use ritual. That's what they've copied."

"Then we rewrite the ritual."

Goldie tilts her head. "You mean mislead them?"

"No," Trixie says. "I mean *test* them. Give them a fold that isn't ours. Let's see if they can carry weight that doesn't belong to them."

The box hums. Not a sound, just a presence. It *knows* the difference.

"Strike price passed," Trixie mutters. "Now we charge interest."

Outside, the wind has changed direction. The third note of the train sounds *before* the first two. Like it's skipping ahead, impatient.

Good.

So are we.

Chapter 65 – Duplicate Keys (Calder Cut)

The Half Pint holds its breath longer these days.

We enter in shifts. Not fear—*calculation*. When someone starts mimicking your rituals, you don't flinch. You measure.

Goldie checks hinges. Lola listens to silence. Trixie watches the bar like it might confess.

The back room's intact, but that's the problem.

It's *too* intact.

Like someone came in, left everything where it was—but made it mean something different.

The kettle's full, cold, and pointed slightly askew. The papers in the archive box haven't been moved—but one has been *considered.* Touched like a cheek, folded like a secret someone hasn't earned.

"Locks untouched," Goldie says.

"They didn't need to break in," Lola replies. "They learned the rhythm. Forged the key from watching us breathe."

Trixie runs a fingertip along the edge of the top sheet. The crease has been read. The paper *knows.*

"Whoever it was," she says, "they're not mocking us. They're *auditioning.*"

Lola's voice lowers. "Calder?"

"Or someone Calder sent," Goldie mutters. "Some poor bastard playing understudy to a man who doesn't forget."

Trixie shuts the lid slowly. "He wants a conversation."

"No," Lola says. "He wants a role."

She crosses to the desk and turns the kettle's spout until it aligns again. Ritual, reclaimed.

Trixie checks the desk drawer. A note. Different paper. Same fold.

Not written by any of us.

Not ours.

She opens it. A single word, written in tidy script, no flourish.

"Soon."

Goldie breathes out through her teeth. "He's not just watching now."

"He's writing," Trixie says. "Mimicking the silence. Contorting it."

Lola doesn't move. "So what do we do?"

"We respond," Trixie says. "Not with panic. With purpose."

She pulls a new sheet from the pad. The good paper. The kind you only use when it counts.

She writes one word.

"No."

She folds it—not quite like we fold ours. Not exactly. Enough to be noticed.

"We leave this," she says, placing it where the other one was.

"And the one he left?" Lola asks.

"We let it travel. Let him think it earned something."

Goldie grins. "That's bait."

"No," Trixie says. "That's credit."

Outside, the train skips its rhythm again—second note, third, then first. Calder's timing.

Let him dance to it.

We've changed the music.

Chapter 66 — Something Off About the Fold

They arrive early, like always. Ritual is rhythm, and rhythm is camouflage. But today, something in the pattern itches.

The door to the Half Pint swings without its usual complaint. The chime is the same, but half a note early, like it was waiting for them.

Lola enters last, slow, eyes on the grain of the floorboards. She doesn't speak, but she doesn't need to—she watches the way a locksmith watches a drawer. Something's been opened, or tried.

Trixie scans the room the way people scan receipts—not for totals, but for what shouldn't be there. The ashtray is clean. Too clean. Goldie peels off her gloves like they said something rude.

"Something off about the fold," Lola murmurs.

She means the room. She means the silence. She means everything.

They sit. The same table, the same orders, but the sugar's been moved. It faces them.

Goldie points. "That wasn't us."

"He watched us," Trixie says. "Then tried to wear us."

Lola opens her notebook. There, in the centre, is a fresh crease. Not hers. Someone tried to fold it. Then changed their mind. She doesn't touch it. She writes nothing. She just lets the crease sit there, like a question.

Behind the bar, the coffee machine hums wrong. It cycles twice, then stops, then starts again. Nervous habit. The machine remembers something it shouldn't.

"This isn't mimicry," Goldie says. "It's audition."

Trixie breathes once through her nose. "Then let's cancel the show."

They don't speak for a while. The noise of the pub moves around them like it's rehearsing. A laugh too loud. A glass clinks once too sharp. Somewhere outside, a bin lid clatters the exact rhythm of a knock.

"The second note was off too," Lola says. "Train didn't hum it right. Sounded... expectant."

Trixie stares at the crease in Lola's notebook. Not touched, but felt. The line where someone else dared to fold.

"He's inside the ritual," Trixie says. "And he doesn't know he's changed it."

Goldie lights a match. Not a cigarette. Just the match. She lets it burn, then drops it into her tea. It hisses. Not a reaction. A punctuation.

"What do we do?" she asks.

Lola closes the notebook, gently, like she's putting someone back to sleep. "We wait. Not for him. For the moment he shows us the fold he *couldn't* copy."

And that's it.

Not silence, but surveillance. Not mimicry, but mutation. Calder's no longer copying them. He's trying to *be* them. And the moment he fails, even slightly, they'll strike.

Because the lock wasn't picked. The duplicate key was copied. But the hand turning it still shakes.

The train hums one note. Misses the second. Swallows the third.

Chapter 67 — Three Ghosts in a Bar

The jukebox isn't playing, but the silence holds a beat.

We're back in the Half Pint, and the light has turned yellow—like the air's been smoking without us. The bar's almost empty except for us and the ghost of a Friday night that never quite happened. The world outside is pretending to be bored. Inside, we're pretending not to count ghosts.

Trixie takes the same stool she always does. Goldie doesn't sit—she leans, one heel hooked on the brass footrail, arms crossed like she's folding in heat. Lola watches the optics with that stare she's perfected—the one that edits liquor into memory.

Behind the bar, the landlord gives us a nod that says, "I've seen worse," and disappears through the back. He knows this crew. He knows the difference between a quiet drink and a quiet reckoning.

"I'm thinking of shaving my head," Trixie says into her glass.

"You're not," Goldie says.

"No," she agrees, "but the idea owes me a drink."

The door opens but no one walks in. Just wind, carrying the kind of cold that remembers who forgot it last. Lola reaches over and shuts it gently, like she's closing a file marked *pending*. The latch clicks like a full stop.

"You hear the train?" Goldie asks.

"Nope," Trixie says. "But I hear the absence."

There's a photo on the wall near the bar. Black-and-white, slightly curled. A trio of strangers laughing like their lives didn't end in courtrooms or car parks. Three men. Three drinks. One joke. We stare at it longer than we should.

Lola tilts her head. "Three ghosts in a bar that forgot how to forget."

We don't answer. We drink instead. It's cheaper than honesty.

On the table between us: a folded receipt, blank side up. No name, no timestamp. Just a crease sharp enough to draw blood.

"We can't keep folding things forever," Goldie says. "Eventually something tears."

"Maybe it's meant to," Trixie replies.

Lola looks at the glass in her hand, and for a moment, it looks back. "There's something in the crease," she says. "Not words. Pressure."

The landlord reappears, wipes the counter like it wronged him, and says nothing. We take that as permission to stay.

Outside, the wind tries again, rattling something loose—a sign, a habit, a name maybe. We don't check.

Inside, silence settles. Not heavy. Not light. Just accurate.

The receipt stays folded.

For now.

Chapter 68 — Keep the Change

The Half Pint doesn't open early, but today the door's unlocked. Not a mistake—an invitation.

No one says rehearsal. No one says anything. Trixie sets the mic like it's a loaded question. Goldie tunes slow, string by string, like she's winding a fuse. Lola sets the chairs—not for comfort, for sightlines. Peggy checks the door twice, then again, the way gamblers pray.

The room smells of floor polish and nerves.

"Sound?" Trixie asks.

"True," Goldie says.

The gear hums in agreement. No feedback. No lies.

Outside, the city shrinks its shoulders. Rain flirts without landing. Calder hasn't shown. But he will. He always arrives for the punchline.

Trixie wears a jacket that doesn't belong to her and boots that do. She hasn't said much since last night—just held Goldie's shirt too long when she handed it back, inside out.

Lola props the bar with a fresh receipt pad. "Tonight," she says, "we don't offer change."

"We never did," Goldie replies.

There's a hush to the setup, like churches before weddings—or wars.

Peggy presses play on a battered tape recorder. Static. Then silence. Then laughter from three nights ago.

She rewinds it without meaning to.

The chalkboard behind the bar has no specials listed—just the word: "Due."

Trixie writes nothing today. No folded notes. No third-hand codes. The ritual has shifted—ink can't carry this part. Only volume.

Goldie leans over. "Still sure?"

Trixie nods. "We give them everything."

"And then?"

"We charge."

The mic hisses once, clears its throat.

It's not time yet. But it's coming. You can feel it in the carpet, in the glassware, in the breath people save without knowing why.

Downstairs, the basement knows. It hums like a withheld confession.

Backstage, the setlist is empty. Doesn't need one. Tonight isn't about memory. It's about reckoning.

Somewhere, Calder's watching. Not from a shadow—those are too honest. He'll come in smiling, like he owns the echo. But he doesn't.

Tonight, they do.

Chapter 69 — The Inhale

The Half Pint feels taller tonight. Like the room itself knows what's coming and is stretching to meet it. Lights are low, but not soft. This isn't mood lighting; it's prelude lighting. The kind that dares you to blink.

Trixie stands near the bar, not touching it. Goldie by the mirror, fixing her collar with the precision of a surgeon. Lola leans against the jukebox, watching the track listing like it might flinch first.

Peggy's name hasn't been spoken yet, but her shadow is here. Someone mentions a new girl. Someone else says, "Don't turn around too fast."

The crew moves like pieces of a ritual, each one folding into place without a word. Shoes get swapped. Lipstick gets reapplied. A black coat is hung, deliberately, on the hook with the bullet hole in it.

"House is full," Goldie says, glancing at the floorboards like she can hear the tension in the nails.

"Not yet it isn't," Trixie says. "But it will be."

Lola says nothing. Just hands Trixie a necklace. The same one from the first night. The one with the broken clasp that still catches light.

Trixie clasps it. Lets it settle.

Outside, the third note of the train hums but doesn't arrive. A promise withheld.

"Any requests?" Goldie asks, half-serious.

"Piece of My Heart," Trixie says, deadpan. "But not yet."

A figure stands by the back wall, unintroduced. Not quite silhouette, not quite memory. She's wearing red, but it doesn't scream. It waits.

The bar hushes itself without being asked.

"One more check," Trixie says.

They each nod, one by one. Not to each other. To the room. To the idea of what comes next.

A flicker of music. Not the song. Just the house system remembering how to breathe.

Goldie slides her hand into Trixie's for a second. Not dalliance. Not declaration. Just pressure. Just there.

And then they wait.

The inhale. Just before the whole place learns to hold its breath.

Chapter 70 — Encore

Back alley behind the Half Pint smells like sweat, menthol, and last chances. The bulb above the stage door flickers like it's got stage fright. Inside, the noise is a nervous thing—people pretending they're not waiting for something. Outside, we know better.

Goldie leans against the bricks, straightens her bra strap with the confidence of someone who's already won the fight. Trixie's shirt is inside out. Deliberate, maybe. Or maybe not. No one's asking.

"Let's not say anything stupid, yeah?" Goldie says, not looking at her.

"Too late," Trixie mutters, tucking the tag into her collar. "We walked in, didn't we?"

Lola appears at the door. Doesn't smile. Doesn't frown. Just nods like she's seen this play before and it still makes her breath catch.

Just as Trixie steps toward the stage, Goldie leans in—not close enough for romance, not far enough for safety—and murmurs, "Make 'em beg, darlin'. But don't give 'em everything."

Trixie doesn't answer. Her smirk does the talking, and her boots finish the sentence.

Inside, the lights dim. The crowd goes that kind of quiet that means they've been drinking just enough to feel things but not enough to forget them.

Trixie walks on stage first. Alone.

She grabs the mic like it owes her something and doesn't give it a second to argue. The band kicks in. The real one. *Piece of My Heart.* No cover, no irony. Just heat.

Her voice doesn't rise—it grabs. It lifts the ceiling. It slaps the bar awake. Goldie joins her on the second verse, harmony sharp as a blade honed on regret. It's not just a song. It's a debt collection.

Peggy is by the bar mouthing every word, like she's praying backwards. Lola doesn't clap. She taps the table once with her ring finger. That's approval. That's church.

When the final beat hits, the crowd erupts. But the girls don't wait for applause.

The lights dip.

Trixie steps forward again. Alone.

No band now. No backup. Just her and a single spotlight that looks like it regrets volunteering.

She sings the slow one. Maybe it was hers. Maybe it was her mother's. Maybe it's no one's but the river's. It's quiet. So quiet a glass cracks near the sink and no one even turns.

Someone coughs halfway through and three strangers look at him like he shot the Queen.

When it ends, no one claps. They just breathe. Together.

She walks off.

On the amp, there's a note. Folded.

Goldie picks it up. Doesn't open it.

"Let it wait," Trixie says. "It knows how."

Outside, the train gives three notes this time. Not two. Not silence.

The street doesn't applaud. But it listens.

The door swings shut behind them. Not slammed. Just final.

A Note to Readers

If something in these pages stayed with you—
a lyric, a name, a silence folded into ritual—then thank you.
Truly.

Books like this don't come with ads or algorithms. They travel by whisper, by accident, by late-night suggestion. If *Middle Name Misery* made you pause, made you fold the corner of a page or play a song louder, I'd be grateful if you'd leave a review. Tell someone. Share it the old-fashioned way.

It's how the notes keep moving.

Until the next one,
Silias

♫ Soundtrack to the Fold

A curated playlist for the quiet wars, the ritual folds, and the fire beneath the silence.

If Middle Name Misery had a heartbeat, this would be its pulse.
Every song here carries the smoke, the silence, the scent of last chances.
Don't shuffle. Don't skip. Just let it play.

1. Elvis Presley – "Trouble"

Theme: Warning shot. The book's DNA.
This is the track the story is *named* after, and it hums under the skin of every silence. It's not background—it's blood.

2. Elvis Presley – "Fever"

Theme: Slow threat. Seduction with intent.
Used when the heat rises but no one moves. It's Peggy's walk, Trixie's stare, Calder's breath.

3. Janis Joplin – "Piece of My Heart"

Theme: Final claim. Trixie and Goldie's duet.
It's not a performance—it's a reckoning. The bar doesn't clap. It pays attention.

4. Mazzy Star – "Into Dust"

Theme: Lola's solo moments.
The chapters where her stillness becomes scripture. Where silence is an inheritance, not absence.

5. Portishead – "Glory Box"

Theme: The crew's rituals, half-dalliances, and heat.
Every folded note, every uncapped pen. Every look that says, *I remember everything but I'm choosing silence*

6. Sharon Van Etten – "Every Time the Sun Comes Up"

Theme: The kitchen scenes.
Tea, bins, MOTs, folded laughter. The sound of real life trying to creep back in.

7. Nick Cave – "Jubilee Street"

Theme: Calder's presence.
When he walks in, he changes the room. He makes silence crawl and notes fold themselves tighter.

8. Agnes Obel – "The Curse"

Theme: The box.
The box that learns. That hesitates. That watches. It hums with this.

9. Amy Winehouse – "Some Unholy War" (stripped)

Theme: Lola again.
Specifically the chapters where she edits her face and the room listens. A track for the unspoken.

10. Dusty Springfield – "I Close My Eyes and Count to Ten"

Theme: The almost-romance.
Goldie's touch. Trixie's silence. That shirt turned inside out. It's not graphic—it's gospel.

11. Chelsea Wolfe – "Feral Love"

Theme: The lead-up to the finale.
The crew on the edge. Folded notes turning into weapons. Rituals becoming law

12. Tom Waits – "Take It With Me"

Theme: The aftermath.
After the last fold. After the note is left unopened. This plays as the street listens.

13. Johnny Flynn – "Detectorists" (Haunted Instrumental)

Theme: The hum.
Whenever the kettle boils but no one drinks. Whenever the river listens.

14. PJ Harvey – "The Words That Maketh Murder"

Theme: The girls' quiet fury.
Not yelling. Just noting. Just planning.

15. Elvis Presley – "City By Night"

Theme: For the streets.
It loops in the background—when Calder walks. When Lola watches. When Southend folds in on itself.

16. Angel Olsen – "Lark"

Theme: The voice Trixie doesn't raise.
A howl that takes its time. A song that folds itself inward before detonating.

17. Fiona Apple – "Under the Table"

Theme: The passive-aggressive showdown chapters.
The ones where politeness is a blade and silence is a snare.

18. Cat Power – "Cross Bones Style"

Theme: Peggy, waiting to strike.
Mouthing words. Ring finger on the table. Knuckle duster unseen, but present.

19. Big Thief – "Not"

Theme: The invoice chapters.
Where the price is listed. And it's not what anyone expected.

20. Leonard Cohen – "The Future"

Theme: The note that stays folded.
A closing track, but it doesn't offer peace. Just warning.

About the Author

Silias Creed is the name stitched into the lining of a coat that never quite fit. Born in the cracks between jukebox songs and shadowed bar booths, Silias writes noir that smells like smoke, sings like trouble, and walks like regret.

He doesn't do readings. He does echoes.

When he isn't unspooling tangled tapes or writing girls who know too much, he's somewhere quiet, listening to the train. Three notes. Never two. Never silence.

You can find him where the river folds.

Coming Soon

Middle Name Misery: The Companion
Folded notes, hidden receipts, unreleased glyphs. The file behind the file. If *Middle Name Misery* was the show, this is the dressing room mirror—with the crack still showing.

How the Web Was Woven
Peggy Harper walks in like she owns the place. Jack Raine follows with a half-smile and a full dossier. This is where the threads start to tighten—and not everyone walks out clean. A new chapter in the *Trixie Vane* series. Spring 2026.

The Silias Creed Cookbook
Recipes from noir kitchens. Comfort food with a sharp tongue. From dripping on toast to bar stool biscuits. Every dish has a story. Every story has a stain. Mid-2026. Bring your own scotch.

Connect with Silias

Got questions, theories, folded notes of your own? Want to argue about which Elvis song should've made the playlist?

Website: www.SiliasCreed.co.uk
Facebook: *Silias Creed — Noir Fiction & Folded Truths*
Radio: The Elvis Radio Show UK – Trixie-approved tunes, B-sides, and barstool confessions.
Buy Me a Scotch: buymeacoffee.com/siliascreed – Support the scrawl, feed the noir.
Email: siliascreed@gmail.com (or shout into a glass of Glenfiddich and hope for the best)

Fold responsibly.

Printed in Dunstable, United Kingdom

72748881R00150